An Interesting Girl

"Charlene's an interesting girl," Marcia Lund said, when Eric drew alongside her on the campground road.

"I think so too. But how did you…"

"No, I mean *interesting*."

Eric's mother had used that word with that emphasis before, sometimes of things she didn't *entirely* approve of. "Mom, c'mon."

Marcia laughed. "She came up to me and introduced herself. Dad came over and she introduced herself again. She said she wanted to meet you. I said you were down on the beach. Then your father invited her to have lunch with us."

Eric grimaced. "Just like Dad." He took an uneasy breath. "Um…will she?"

"If her parents don't object. And why would they?" Marcia grabbed her son's forearm and squeezed it.

Eric waved her hand away. "Ok, ok. Now, what makes her, um, *interesting?*"

"Everything she said, she said in complete sentences. You could learn a few things from her."

Eric groaned. "You're an English teacher even on summer vacation."

"I get paid year-round. And my kids will *not* be illiterate."

They left the road and rounded the family's big blue tent.

Charlene was already sitting at the campsite picnic table across from Eric's younger sister Lisa, with a bright orange Melmac plate in front of her and a very big grin on her face.

Complete Sentences

Complete Sentences

Jeff Duntemann

Copperwood Press • Scottsdale, Arizona
2021

Complete Sentences

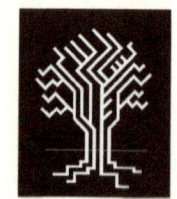

Copperwood Media, LLC

Scottsdale, Arizona

For Kathy Stumpf, sister-in-law and friend,
who understands the hearts and minds of grade schoolers
as only a dedicated grade-school teacher can.

1

August 13, 1966

Eric Lund stood on the sand shore of Castle Rock Lake, compass in hand, scoping out the eastern horizon. There was a conjunction of Mars and Jupiter in Gemini before sunrise, and he would need a good eastern horizon to see both planets well. A telescope would *really* help...but he didn't have one.

Yet. His parents had promised him the optics for a reflecting telescope for his 13th birthday, still almost a year off. He'd been poring over a couple of library books now for months, teaching himself how such telescopes worked, and sketching out what he could build with the scrap lumber, pipe fittings, and odd junk in the crawlspace. By this time next year, with any luck at all, it would be finished. If the horizons were right, he'd ask his parents to come back to this campground. Wisconsin night skies were spectacular. He was looking forward to seeing how well Castle Rock Lake skies compared to others he had visited.

He heard sand crunching behind him. Eric turned. A girl was walking toward him. He recognized her as the girl he'd seen with the family in the tent site next over, while he'd helped his father put up his own family's large blue tent. She was his age or close, a head shorter in bare feet, dark brown hair past her shoulders, wearing denim shorts and a Batman T-shirt. She had wide brown eyes and a dazzling smile.

A pretty girl, wow, smiling at *him*. He smiled back and tried to seem nonchalant. Not necessarily easy, with a compass in one hand and a planisphere in the other. As usual, the Mad Scientist of St. James School was caught in the act.

"Hi!" she called before closing the last few yards between them. She had a deep summer tan and freckles across the bridge of her nose. "I'm Charlene. My family's camped next to yours. What are you looking for?"

Eric held up the compass. "Due east," he said, because it was as close to the truth as he could manage in his current situation. The compass would tell him…

Charlene pivoted on the sand and pointed across the lake to a water tower in the distance.

Eric tucked the planisphere under one arm and laid the compass flat on his palm. Well, due east was a couple of degrees to the left of the water tower, but…

"Bingo. Thanks! Um, I'm Eric. Eric Lund."

"Charlene Sawyer. You've got Illinois plates. Chicago?"

"Arlington Heights. Close enough."

"What's that?" She tapped on the edge of the planisphere.

Eric tucked the compass in his pants pocket and held the planisphere in both hands. "It's a kind of slide rule that helps you locate the constellations." He nudged the top disk around the center pivot with his thumb. "If you line up the time you're looking at the sky with the current date, the map disk shows you where the stars are." After lining up August 13th with 9:30 PM, Eric proffered her the planisphere. She took it, turning it until the East marker on the top disk aligned with the water tower, and spent long seconds looking down at the oval window showing the night sky.

"Got it. Neat! Lyra's right there in the middle! I've seen it in books but I've never actually *seen* it."

Eric swallowed hard. A girl his age who liked astronomy? What were the *chances?* "Um, Lyra will be out tonight when it gets dark. I can show you where."

"You would?" Charlene's face lit up with delight. "For me?"

"Well, sure. It's easy. Right from here on the beach. Saturn will be out too." Eric looked again at the water tower. "How did you know the water tower is due east?"

Charlene shrugged. "They had a nature hike here a couple of years ago, and the guide told us. They had the hike last year too, and the guide told us again."

"You must come here a lot."

"Every year, the middle two weeks of August. It's a family tradition."

"Eric! Lunch! Kielbasa!" Eric looked toward the campground road, where his mother was standing, hands to her mouth.

Eric waved and started walking toward the road.

Charlene followed. "What time tonight? I have to ask my folks. I'm supposed to be back at our site by dark."

Eric looked off to one side for a moment, doing the ecliptic math in his head. "We're seven weeks past the solstice, so… nine should be dark enough." He stopped. "Do you think your folks will let you?" He was surprised at how much he feared the wrong answer.

"My dad will. He wants me to be interested in science. Mom would rather I not even talk to a boy until I'm 16. But she defers to him. I'm optimistic." Charlene darted off toward her family's campsite.

By the time Eric reached the road, his mother was already headed back to their campsite. He had to trot to catch up.

"Charlene's an interesting girl," Marcia Lund said, when Eric drew alongside her on the campground road.

"I think so too. But how did you know…"

"No, I mean *interesting*."

Eric's mother had used that word with that emphasis before, sometimes of things she didn't entirely approve of. "Mom, c'mon."

Marcia laughed. "She came up to me and introduced herself. Dad came over and she introduced herself again. She said she wanted to meet you. I said you were down on the beach. Then your father invited her to have lunch with us."

Eric grimaced. "Just like Dad." He took an uneasy breath. "Um…will she?"

"If her parents don't object. And why would they?" Marcia grabbed her son's forearm and squeezed it.

Eric waved her hand away. "Ok, ok. Now, what makes her, um, *interesting?*"

"Everything she said, she said in complete sentences. You could learn a few things from her."

Eric groaned. "You're an English teacher even on summer vacation."

"I get paid year-round. And my kids will *not* be illiterate."

They left the road and rounded the family's big blue tent.

Charlene was already sitting at the campsite picnic table across from Eric's younger sister Lisa, with a bright orange Melmac plate in front of her and a very big grin on her face.

2

"Grab a bun, kids!" Jack Lund said, handing the basket of hot dog rolls to Eric. "Fresh out of the bag. Can't pound nails with 'em yet, so they're good eatin'." Eric placed a roll on Charlene's plate and one on his own, and passed the basket to his sister. Marcia walked around the table with a plate of sizzling Harczak's Polish Sausage and a fork, stabbing and placing one sausage on each roll. A chop suey carton of coleslaw went around next, followed by a large bag of potato chips. Jack popped a bottle of Coke for each of them.

Six-year-old Lisa did her best with the coleslaw, but fumbled the serving spoon and dumped some in her lap on and the edge of the table.

"*Śvinka!*" Marcia scolded, grabbing a handful of paper towels to mop up her daughter.

"That means 'little pig' in Polish," Lisa said, and then, quietly, "I have to be more careful."

With all plates full and both parents seated, Marcia began the Sign of the Cross. Charlene did her best to imitate Marcia's example, her brow wrinkled in concentration. Oh—she wasn't Catholic. To Eric that was an odd notion. All his friends were from St. James Parish. Charlene bowed her head and closed her eyes while the Lunds recited the prayer itself.

Bless us, O Lord, and these thy gifts,
Which we are about to receive, from thy bounty,
Through Christ our Lord, Amen!

"Amen," Charlene said, and this time, when the family made the Sign of the Cross, she made it with them.

Jack raised a bottle of Blatz to his lips. "Dig in! And glad you could join us, Charlene!"

Eric dug into his kielbasa. Charlene took a bite and chewed slowly and deliberately. "This is wonderful! I've never had kielbasa before." She took another bite, the lights coming up in her face. "Mrs. Lund, do you speak Polish?"

"*Tak*," Marcia said.

"That means 'yes,'" Lisa whispered.

"Lisa, shush," Marcia said. "My parents married at 16 and came over from Krakow in 1913. My father never mastered English. Eric knows a little from talking to them, though he needs to work on his pronunciation."

"Mom—"

Charlene set down her kielbasa."How do you say, 'Thank you' in Polish?"

"*Dziękuję.*"

"Mr. Lund, Mrs. Lund, gin-koo-ya, for having me." Charlene had done her best, and Eric gave her big credit. He didn't do as well sometimes, but his grandparents, unlike his mother, were patient. The Polish word for "rat" still tied his throat in knots. He suspected his mother talked about rats during his impromptu Polish lessons just to razz him.

"*Nie ma za co.* You're always welcome here."

Table conversation was sparse until the kielbasas were gone. Eric had seconds. Charlene did not. Eric's father encouraged her to talk about herself without asking outright for her life story. Jack Lund was a master of conversation, and Rule #1 for dinner-table talk was "Everybody speaks and everybody listens." Rule #2, enforced without mercy by Eric's mother, was "Everybody uses correct English."

In Charlene's perfect English and complete sentences, they learned that the Sawyers lived in Janesville, Wisconsin; that Charlene was twelve, and a month older than Eric; that her sister Marianne was nine; that her father James was a professor of chemistry at Blackhawk Technical College; and that she and Marianne were homeschooled by their mother Claire—with occasional chemistry lessons from their father.

"My dad wants me to be a pharmacist, like my grandfather was," Charlene explained. "So he has us drawing atoms and molecules all the time, and memorizing things like isotopes. I don't tell him so, but it's a little boring."

Jack picked a potato chip out of the bag, and chewed thoughtfully. "So…what would you rather be?"

Charlene squirmed on her chair, her smile fading out after a few seconds. "I want to be a commercial artist. If they'll let me. My father thinks artists starve."

"You're an *artist?*" little Lisa asked, sitting up straight, with an expression Eric knew was awe.

"I am!" Charlene reached back and pulled a small spiral notebook from her back pocket, along with a pencil stub the length of her little finger. She flipped to a new page, and, with her eyes on Lisa, began drawing. Eric watched from Charlene's side, sharing his sister's awe, while Charlene sketched Lisa with deft strokes. In just a little more than a minute, Charlene tore the sheet free of the spiral, and handed it across the table to Lisa.

Lisa held the sheet in both hands with something like reverence, and stared at it for long seconds. "Nobody ever drawed me before!"

"Drew, honey," Marcia said. "Say, 'Nobody ever drew me before.'"

"Nobody ever drew me before." She looked at Charlene. "That's *really* true."

"Hold it up, Lisa," Jack said. Lisa turned the little portrait toward her father and held it high. "That's fine work, Charlene! And I know some commercial artists. I work for a big insurance company downtown. Two floors up is our publications department. Five or six artists do flyers and manuals and underwriting tables and things. They have offices bigger than mine! If they're starving up there I haven't heard about it."

Marcia stood and began collecting dirty plates and paper napkins.

"Wow! That's *so* cool!" Charlene took the bag of potato chips and shook a few more onto her other hand. In a low voice she added, "My parents won't let me eat these at home."

"We won't tell anybody!" Jack said, laughing, and popped another beer for himself. "Art's a good business. I actually met Marcia in art class back in college. She was the pretty girl at the front of the class that we were all drawing."

"And I was *not* naked, you goof!" She poked him playfully in the ribs, then set the plates down and gave him a quick hug from behind.

"Did I say you were?"

"Thanksgiving dinner, 1964? Hmmm?"

"She was wearing a swimsuit," Lisa said, just a little above a whisper.

Eric cringed. He'd heard that story so many times in so many variations—most involving significant quantities of beer—that it didn't much register anymore…except that a *girl* was sitting next to him.

Marcia took up the stack of plates again, and waved them toward the plastic basin on the open tailgate of their Impala wagon. "Eric. Dish duty."

Eric nodded. "I have chores for a bit," he said to Charlene.

Charlene stood. *"Dziękuję* to all of you!" she called. Her pronunciation was almost perfect. *How did she do that?* Eric wondered, watching her thread her way between the pines back toward her family's campsite.

3

August had been hot—but September meant school. It was a tradeoff Eric was willing to make. He tore a long blade of grass from the turf in the big field across the road from the family tent, held it at arm's length, and dropped it. The blade wriggled straightaway back to Earth. The air was humid and close, but calm—perfect glider weather. Before today, he would never have thought that flying a glider might attract a girl's attention. Eric glanced toward the tents, across the road around the edge of the field. But before today, well, he had not met Charlene.

He slumped his haversack off his back and pulled out the glider Uncle Louie had given him for his 12th birthday in May. The wings and fuselage were two separate pieces, made of a near-miraculous sort of plastic. Countless little white beads were squirted into a mold, where they expanded and hardened into something that was very rugged (compared to balsa wood) but amazingly light. It helped that Uncle Louie worked in a plastics factory, sure. But his uncle was right: This put balsa gliders to shame.

Eric slid the wing into a matching slot in the side of the fuselage. He gently pushed the plane into the air, watching it carefully as it flew a few yards to make sure the wings were dead-on straight. They were. That done, he dug the launcher out of his haversack. Nothing special, just a wooden handle with a long quarter-inch rubber band fastened to one end. He hooked the rubber band into a matching notch under the glider's nose, aimed at the sky, pulled the glider back until the band was taut, and then let it go.

The glider arrowed almost straight up, then gracefully arced and began its slow, spiral descent. It circled nine times before hitting the grass gently and going nose-down. Eric began walking toward the landing point, probably fifty feet toward the tents.

"Eric! Eric!" Charlene ran across the field, her moccasins in her hand. They closed on the white glider at about the same time. "That was...*beautiful!*"

"Yup," he said, picking up the glider. "This is a good one."

"Can I try it?"

"Sure."

"Show me how."

Eric offered her the glider. "Hand-toss first. There's no wind right now, so it doesn't matter which way you face. If there's a breeze, face into the wind. Hold the glider where it balances in your hand." Charlene gently pinched the glider between her thumb and forefinger, her face crinkled up in concentration. She nudged the glider forward and back with her left hand.

Eric hesitated before speaking. He wasn't used to explaining things like this. "No. Use your thumb and three fingers."

"Which three fingers?"

He took a deep breath. Gliders showed better than they told. He could make her grip perfect in a few seconds, tops. But... that would mean...

"Eric, what's wrong?"

"Um, I'm kind of messing this up." He coughed into his elbow. "Ok. Hold the glider at shoulder height. Use whatever fingers work for you. It's not magic."

Eric moved a half step behind Charlene. He placed his right hand over hers, and could feel the tension in her slender fingers. Eric slipped his fingertips between her fingers to spread them out along the fuselage of the glider. Her skin was warm, soft, almost velvety.

"That's good, that's good," he said, making sure she had the balance point.

"I think it *is* magic," Charlene whispered, and squeezed his fingertips between her splayed fingers.

Eric closed his eyes for a few seconds, reveling in her touch while trying to puzzle it all out. What was going on? He had danced with his cousin Mary Catherine at her big sister's wedding back in June. One of his hands held one of hers, the other was on her waist. Sure, it was fun, but it wasn't…this.

This. Charlene backed up until her shoulder touched Eric's ribs. Eric withdrew his hand from Charlene's. "Now gently toss forward, keeping the glider level."

Tongue between her teeth, Charlene rocked her hand forward and released the glider. It flew at chin height for almost thirty feet, before landing belly-down.

"Perfect!" Eric shouted.

"Yowie!" Charlene replied, running on bare feet to retrieve the glider. When she got to it, she picked it up and turned back toward Eric. "Let's play catch!"

"You're on!"

Charlene again found the glider's balance point, and pushed it forward into the air with more force than she had the first time. Her aim was true; Eric had to walk no more than ten feet to reach up and pluck it out of the air. Without saying a word he balanced it and sent it back toward her, a little higher than before. Charlene leapt with more grace than Eric expected, and caught the glider at least seven feet off the ground.

Eric clapped. "You're a pro!"

"This is fun! Here comes!" She sent the plane back toward Eric with more force. Eric jumped and missed it, and trotted another thirty feet to where the glider touched down.

Charlene put her hands to her mouth. "I'm sorry!"

"Don't be sorry! That was a great toss!" Eric sent the glider back toward Charlene across an even greater distance. Charlene ran fast, jumped, and snatched it out of the air, laughing.

For twenty minutes the glider flew back and forth between them, sometimes caught in mid-flight, sometimes missed and retrieved from the grass. As Charlene ran to catch it the last time, she yipped and stumbled to the ground, holding one foot in both hands. "I stepped on something!"

Eric ran to her and sat beside her. She took her hands away from her foot and inspected her sole for damage. She'd lost a little skin. Small drops of blood appeared down the length of a scrape that was at least two inches long. Eric got up and followed what he remembered of her path, scanning for anything that might break the skin if stepped on. *Aha!* He bent down in the scrubby grass, dug a little with his index finger, and came up with a piece of broken red-clay drain pipe. Part of one ragged edge had been protruding from the soil. Not a rusty nail, at least.

Eric sat. Charlene looked briefly at the clay fragment in his hands and waved it away.

"Mom's going to be mad."

Eric scolded himself internally for causing her to hurt herself. "You should maybe wear your shoes when we do this."

Her eyes went distant, beyond him. "I go barefoot because mom hates it when I do."

"She's just trying to keep you from getting hurt."

"No. She thinks feet are ugly. Her toes are all bent up. It's those stupid pointy high heels she wears. She complains how much they hurt her, but she keeps wearing them."

Eric had no clear idea how to respond to that. "Um, we have Band-Aids and Merthiolate in our first-aid kit. And I got my

First Aid merit badge this spring. You stay here. I'll get the kit and fix it up."

Charlene managed a wan smile. "Don't get in trouble for my sake."

"Trouble? No way. My dad leaned on me to get the First Aid badge. He had it when he was in Scouts. Stay there."

The campsite was quiet. Eric's mom had taken Lisa to the playground near the campground entrance. His father was in a camp chair, reading, his feet up on the picnic bench seat. Eric had to dig a little in the back seat of the Impala to find the first-aid kit, and wondered if he could get past his father's notice.

No chance. Jack put his book down on one thigh, its pages splayed to keep the place. "Ok. What happened?"

"Charlene scraped her foot on a piece of broken clay pipe. Her feet are dirty and I don't want the scrape to get infected."

"Hmmm. Did she break the skin?"

"Not like a cut. Scraped it some. A little blood. I've had lots worse."

"Good man." His father pointed at the roll of paper towels on the table. "Wipe it with peroxide and dish soap. Don't use a Band-Aid; they don't stick to feet. Use a gauze pad. And—"

"Dad, c'mon. I know all that."

"Sure. Because I taught you. But a refresher never hurts." Jack Lund grinned. "She's worth it, right?"

Eric felt his face flush. "Um, yeah. She is." Some days he thought his father would never understand him. This day was not one of them. Eric tore off several paper towels and set out for the field, kit in hand. "Thanks, dad."

Charlene's feet were filthy. Eric didn't consider himself a paragon of cleanliness, but he wondered if he had ever gotten his feet that black. He pulled a small squeeze bottle of dish detergent from the kit. The bottle of peroxide provided a little water for the green gobbet of detergent pressed out onto a paper towel. He gently swabbed the bottom of Charlene's right foot. She winced. The towel came away black.

"Hurts?" he asked.

"A little."

"I'll be careful."

"No," she said. "Do a good job. I don't care of it hurts."

"*I* care if it hurts."

Eric swabbed several more times, balancing the pressure on her skin with a sense that the grime was coming away on the towel. Once her skin looked clean, he swapped in a fresh towel and wiped the scrape once more with peroxide. "Halfway there," he said.

The next part would be the worst. Eric unscrewed the cap of the Merthiolate bottle and held it close to the scrape. He daubed the purple liquid onto the wound. Charlene jumped. She clamped her hands around her foot above and below the cut and grit her teeth. One more daub—and another jump—and Eric put the little bottle away.

"Almost done." The first-aid kit provided a gauze pad, bandage, and tape. When the Merthiolate had dried, he pressed the gauze pad against the scrape and wrapped it with the bandage, across her sole and up around her instep, taping it to keep it in place

"Ok. That's it." Eric picked up her right moccasin. "Um, will you wear your shoes if I ask you to?"

Charlene nodded, suddenly grinning. "Of course I will. You saved my sole!" She laughed, and Eric laughed, picking up her other moccasin. He had brought it toward her left foot when he noticed that she had a small, tattered, and mostly black Band-Aid wrapped around her little toe.

"Um, that Band-Aid is on its last legs. I have lots here. Let me wrap a new one for you."

A frown flashed across Charlene's face. Slowly her smile returned, and she nodded.

As gently as he could, Eric gripped the coming-loose edge of the dirty Band-Aid and pulled. It came away without much resistance. Eric caught his breath. Her toenail was bright red.

"What did you do…oh! Nail polish."

Charlene twisted around and scanned the tents on the other side of the road. "Please cover it up again. I don't want mom to see it."

Eric wrapped a clean Band-Aid around her little toe, making sure it was snug and unlikely to slip off.

They locked eyes for long seconds. Then Charlene pulled on her left moccasin and tucked her feet beneath her. "I can't explain right now. Really. But if mom sees it, I'm in trouble."

Eric shrugged. He reached back to the first-aid kit and pulled out three more Band-Aids. "Spares," he said. "Just in case."

Charlene took the proffered Band-Aids and tucked them into a pocket in her shorts. "You're good for me," she said, her eyes twinkling. "Thanks."

Eric rose and trotted across the field to where the glider was, picked it up, and returned. As he sat down, Charlene reached for the glider in his hands. She turned it around in front of her eyes, looking at every part of it. "This glider belongs to the air," she said.

"Huh?" He suspected she was changing the subject. That was ok. Eric hadn't much liked their previous subject.

"It does. Without the air it wouldn't be a glider."

"Um, I don't follow."

"Suppose you were on the Moon. You would toss the glider, and it would just fall down. Like a rock."

Eric nodded. "Without air, a glider might as well be a rock."

"But with the air…it's a glider. It *flies*. It belongs to the air."

"Um, but the air doesn't own it…"

Charlene set the glider down. She caught his eyes, and there was pain in her expression. Her foot? Or…"Belonging isn't about being owned. It's about being home."

Eric wasn't quite sure what to make of that, so he snapped the first-aid kit closed. He picked up the kit and the glider and got to his feet. Charlene smiled almost all the time. Now she wasn't smiling. Something was wrong somewhere, but he had no idea how to ask what it might be, and even less idea how to comfort her.

Charlene pushed against the ground to get one foot under her, then fell back, grimacing. She reached up with her right hand. Eric took it, and helped her to stand. The feeling of her hand in his was still magical. They walked slowly back to the tents, Charlene favoring one leg, and occasionally wincing from the pain.

When Eric and Charlene rounded the side of his family's tent, Charlene stopped, grasping Eric's upper arm to steady herself. At the picnic table, Eric's parents were sitting with another man, drinking coffee and laughing.

"That's my dad," Charlene said under her breath.

Eric urged her forward. She dropped onto the picnic table bench and pulled off one moccasin.

"Hey, Shar, you're limping," Mr. Sawyer said.

"I stepped on something out on the field."

"Well, shoes exist for a reason."

Eric thought it was kind of a cold thing for a father to say when his daughter was in pain. The silence was about as awkward as any Eric had endured in some time. Charlene would not look at her father.

Mr. Sawyer broke the silence. He came around the table and extended his hand. "Eric. James Sawyer." Eric shook his large hand. "I've been talking to your folks—your father and I were both in Italy during the War. In fact, we were both at Monte Cassino, but half the Americans in Italy were there too. Claire and I would like you to join us for supper. I cleared it with your parents. What do you think?"

"Yessir. I'd be delighted." It still sounded a little strange to Eric, but it was...*manners*. And manners mattered in the Lund household. "Thank you very much for having me."

"Our pleasure. 5:30?"

"Yessir. 5:30 would be fine."

Mr. Sawyer turned to Charlene, and grasped her arm beneath her right shoulder. "Time to come home and get the weight off that foot, kiddo. You need to do a little healing."

He helped her up, and Charlene limped beside him back toward their campsite.

4

The rest of the afternoon seemed to drag on forever. Eric sat at the picnic table, sketching his future telescope on the brown grocery bag his mother had emptied to begin preparing supper. If Charlene had been impressed by a plastic glider, how much more would she be impressed by a telescope that could show her the moons of Jupiter? Could he persuade his father to bring them back to this campground sometime the middle of next August?

Too early to worry about *that*—though it didn't stop him from worrying. The pencil returned to his sketch. Were there enough pipe fittings in the gunny sack he had rescued from his grandma's garage? The little ones would be of no use. He needed the big, 2" size. Mass meant stability, so…Eric looked up, wondering if Charlene's foot were still hurting her.

Focus, he ordered his wandering mind. Eric had the library's copy of Jean Texereau's *How to Make a Telescope* opened to the blueprints for a square tube made out of plywood. Plywood! There were stacks of plywood scraps in the crawlspace from when his father and uncle had finished the basement. And his telescope would belong to the stars, because without the stars, it would just be a bunch of screwed-together wood scraps—

"Eric, I think you should put the library book away." His mother was tending a pot of stew on the camp stove. Eric smelled onions and just-now-cut carrots, plus the beef he had diced last night at his mother's direction. She pointed toward their tent. "It's going to get messy here. If you ruin the book, well, you know what happens."

He snapped the book shut and looked down. Last summer he'd left a book on the constellations out in the rain, and had paid the library seven dollars for it out of his money jar. It had been a huge lesson in taking care of things. Was that why he'd wanted to fix Charlene's foot himself? More such questions were bubbling up all the time. The girl was pushing everything else out of his head.

Marcia shook a glug of red wine into the stew pot, and twisted the flour sifter above it. She added shakes from several small bottles and cans of spices.

The stew had been underway for an hour or so. By now it had to be five o'clock. Only half an hour more…

Eric ducked into the tent and put the book into his haversack. He paused beside his sleeping bag and little suitcase of clothes. Charlene's hand had felt no different from his cousin's hand at the wedding. So it wasn't about her hand. What, then, was it about? Her smile? Her large brown eyes just seemed to *sparkle*.

Eric shook his head, trying to think about telescopes. He'd have one someday. In the meantime, tonight he would show Charlene the constellations…

"Eric!" his mother called.

He pushed back the tent flap. Beside his mother was a girl in a denim jumper with short blond hair, eight or nine. Eric stepped out of the tent, puzzled.

"Eric, this is Marianne Sawyer, Charlene's sister. Her father sent her over to fetch you for supper. Charlene's trying not to walk much." Once he got within range, his mother reached up with both hands to smooth down his disorderly hair. "You've got a comb somewhere. I think it's high time you got in the habit of using it."

Marianne walked in silence beside him until they got to the road. The girl looked over her shoulder, then stepped closer to Eric. "Are you Charlene's boyfriend now?" she asked, just above a whisper.

Eric twitched. "Um, I just met her this morning."

"Well, she had lunch with your family. You're having dinner with us. You fixed up her foot. And she's been talking about you all afternoon."

Apprehension pushed reverie out of his head. "Talking about me? What did she say?" The questions came out machine-gun fast.

"That you have a cardboard compass that shows where the stars are, and you're building a big telescope. She said your dad is really funny, and your mom speaks Polish." Marianne dropped her voice still further. "She said she wished it wasn't so far to Chicago."

Eric had had that same wish over lunch.

Marianne then spoke in a whisper. "I think she really likes you. She didn't say that, exactly, but I can tell. She won't say it in front of my mom. They don't always get along. This is a secret, ok?"

"Yup. Our secret." Something about Marianne's words seemed a little off. *She won't say it in front of my mom.* Why not "our mom?"

At that point Marianne left the road, near her family's gray tent. Mr. Sawyer was standing by the site's picnic table, waving. Charlene was looking their way, her smile present, if—in some weird way, Eric thought—struggling.

Eric, glad you could join us." Mrs. Sawyer patted the picnic bench place across from Charlene. She was short and heavy, with blonde hair cut pretty much the way Marianne's hair was cut. In fact, she looked a lot like a stouter, grown-up version of Marianne. Eric slid onto the spot she had indicated.

Charlene looked heartbroken. "Mom, can't he sit next to me? I got to sit next to him at lunch."

"But this way he can look at you, honey."

Charlene looked pleadingly at her father. "Dad?"

James Sawyer waved his hands in the air. "Claire, it's all right, really." He turned to Eric, pointing at the spot beside Charlene. "Go ahead, Eric. Sit wherever you want. We have lots of room."

Eric got up and crossed the table around Mr. Sawyer, to sit at Charlene's right. Mrs. Sawyer turned away without speaking. On a folding table beside their camp stove were three empty cans of Dinty Moore beef stew. On the camp stove was a pot over a low flame sending up curls and rosettes of steam. Mrs. Sawyer stirred the pot with a long wooden spoon. So Eric was having stew tonight anyway—and hoped his expert-cook mother never found out what kind of stew it actually was.

Mrs. Sawyer served the meal almost entirely in silence. She poured glasses of water for Eric, Charlene, and Marianne, and coffee from a battered percolator pot for herself and Mr. Sawyer. Eric thought that her next step was peculiar: She opened both ends of a husky can of something called "date nut bread," and pushed on one end of the dark brown bread inside. As the bread protruded from the other end of the can, she cut neat round slices with a sharp knife and stacked them on a paper plate.

Canned bread, wow. It was the sort of thing that would make his own mother start muttering in Polish. Mrs. Sawyer set out salt and pepper and a butter dish, and laid a paper napkin on a three-section paper plate in front of each of them. That done, she retrieved the pot of stew from the stove and ladled a dollop of stew onto each plate.

"Claire, thank you," James said, and waved his wife to her place at the table. "Eric, we don't talk much at meals so we can enjoy the peace and quiet. It helps us unwind at the end of the day."

Eric found himself tense in spite of having been welcomed by Charlene's parents. In his experience, silence at mealtime suggested that people were angry at one another. He was pretty sure it wasn't the case here, and only began to relax when Charlene took her first fork full of steaming stew. He followed her lead.

"Still, we'd like to get to know you a little better. Charlene says you're interested in the sciences."

Eric swallowed hurriedly. "Yessir. I am. I always have been. Astronomy especially."

Mr. Sawyer took a slice of the strange round canned bread and spread some butter on it. "Do you see a career path there?"

Career path? Eric guessed that that meant a job. Eric didn't think of astronomy in those terms. He and his father had discussed the responsibility inherent in having a job, but the jobs they talked about were things like washing dishes at restaurants. Looking at the stars was just…fun. He wasn't sure who would pay him real money to do it.

"Nossir, not really," Eric said, with a creeping sense of dread that it was the wrong answer. Perhaps it was better to steer the conversation in another direction—politely, of course. "My dad works for Colfax Insurance. They have a career day downtown every year for employee kids twelve and up. I went in May. My dad introduced me to the man who manages the company's computers. He spent an hour with me, and explained how computers work. He even took the panels off one to show me what was inside. That was extremely interesting."

Mr. Sawyer smiled, nodding. "Computers, yes. It *is* an interesting field, a form of applied math. We have an IBM 1130 at the college, and the Dean of Sciences would like to lease one of the big System/360 units that IBM started delivering last year, if we can get some budget for it. If the Dean gets us a System/360, he says he'll put together a degree program. I wish

I knew more about it myself. I will grant that it's a growing industry. I'm sure there will be jobs there in a few years, if not immediately."

Eric decided to try the date nut bread. The butter was really margarine and the bread more like cake than bread, but he watched how Charlene used her slice to soak up the juice from the stew on her plate, and did the same. "Mr. Marwick at Colfax Insurance told me that by 1974, computers wouldn't be any larger than a clothes washer. He thinks there will be thousands of new jobs by the time I'm finished with college in 1976."

Mr. Sawyer smiled what seemed a slightly pained smile. "A smart man is *never* finished with college."

At that point silence again fell, with Eric feeling like he hadn't provided quite the answers that the Sawyers expected. Mr. and Mrs. Sawyer finished their stew, and Claire rose to serve everyone a little more. She sat down again, an uncomfortable expression on her face. She was looking all around Eric but not at him, and seemed to be struggling for something to say.

"Well, Eric, thank you for coming to supper. You're very mature and have excellent table manners." Although she was smiling, Eric thought he caught a slight tremble at the corners of her mouth during the long seconds before she spoke again. "Does your mother allow you to go to mixed parties?"

"Claire, really," Mr. Sawyer said.

Mixed parties. Girls. *Uh-oh.* Eric decided to jump in before things got any worse. "No ma'am. Or…I don't really know. I've never been invited to any."

Charlene was staring down at her empty plate. She looked miserable.

"Do you have a lot of friends who are girls? I mean friends— not girlfriends, of course, at your age."

"Claire…"

What could he do but ride it out, and hope he said the right things? "Um, no ma'am. Our school emphasizes academics, and I take them seriously. The girls I would like to have as friends also take their academics seriously. This doesn't leave much time for us to talk to each other."

Eric didn't like lying to grownups. The real truth was that the girls in his class thought he was strange, and made fun of the way he talked.

"What qualities do you think you would like in a girlfriend someday?"

"Claire. Enough!" Mr. Sawyer turned to Eric. "Eric, when you take Charlene down to the beach tonight to see the constellations, I'd like you to take Marianne as well. I'll bet she would enjoy seeing them."

"Yes, please!" Marianne said. "I can see the stars, but I can never draw the lines!"

Whew. Eric felt like he had somehow dodged some truly weird calamity. He relaxed, at least a little. "Yessir, of course. I'd be glad to. In fact, if you and Mrs. Sawyer would like to come as well, I'd love to tour the sky with all of you!"

Charlene kicked Eric's ankle. Hard.

Mr. Sawyer drained the last of his coffee. "Thanks, but I think we'll stay here. We don't talk much at meals, but we *do* talk."

Now it was Mrs. Sawyer who was staring down at her plate.

Charlene took another slice of date nut bread, spread margarine all over it, and handed it to Eric. He got the message, and the rest of the meal was spent in the Sawyers' accustomed silence.

5

Three flashlight beams lit the campground road. With Charlene to his right and Marianne to his left, Eric led the way to where the road swung toward the lake and the sand came right up to the crumbling edges of the asphalt. A slow breeze like a soft warm breath came off the lake, heavy with the scent of summer, and gentle water sounds joined with the August cricket song. Charlene's left hand gripped Eric's right arm just below the end of his T-shirt sleeve. Her touch was still magical, perhaps moreso because she was putting her weight on his arm whenever she took a step. She could walk because he was there to help. He tried to drive the thought out of his head, but with each tightening of Charlene's hand on his bare arm, the intoxicating thought returned: *She needs me!*

The trio walked out onto the beach until they had gone midway across the sand, within several yards of the water. Eric scanned the horizon. "This should be good, right here."

Charlene squeezed his arm one last time, and pulled herself against him. She tipped her head until her temple touched his shoulder. "Thank you," she whispered.

"Whatever I can do to help," he whispered in reply. He looked up again as she drew away. "Turn off your flashlights." The three lights flicked out, leaving them in darkness.

No one moved nor spoke as their flashlight-dazzled eyes gradually adapted. Above them, in an order Eric had witnessed under many dark Wisconsin skies since he'd been a small boy, the stars were coming out. First, the brightest of the brilliant: Antares, Spica, Vega, Deneb, Altair, all torches of the night. And one more, in their league but not of their kind: Saturn, a steadfast untwinkling pale yellow in the southeast. As his eyes grew more accustomed to the dark, the second-string stars appeared. Eric could name some but not all, and they were everywhere, the framing members of the constellations, not torches but—he grinned—two by fours. Soon after emerged the multitudes of lesser magnitudes, down to the limits of his eyes to discern. Finally, meandering down the sky toward Sagittarius in the south, a river of pale stardust, the Milky Way.

"Wow!" Marianne said to his left. "I'm lost already!"

Charlene tsked. "Nobody's lost with Eric around."

"Especially you," Marianne muttered.

It was a girl thing; Eric guessed that he wouldn't understand. He shrugged, and knelt beside Marianne. "We'll start right here. Turn toward the north." He gripped Marianne's hand and pulled her around until she was facing the same way he was. He noted that there was no magic in Marianne's hand, as there was in Charlene's. "Right over the trees in the north. Look hard. You'll see the Big Dipper."

He felt her hand tense. "Yes! It's there! I see it! It's really big!"

"Yup. That's why it's not called The Medium-Sized Dipper. Now look at the bowl of the Dipper. Find the two stars at its left side."

"I see them."

"Now draw a straight line between those two stars, and extend it upward until the line hits another star."

Marianne remained silent for a few seconds. If she had never looked up at a sky as crisp and clear as this, she might have trouble separating the Dipper's canonical stars from the clutter of fainter lights everywhere around them. So he was patient. She was only nine.

Charlene placed her hand on his shoulder and squeezed twice. Eric suspected she was thanking him for catering to her bratty little sister. Again, he felt Marianne's hand tense as her eyes learned the skill of separating the brighter lights from the fainter.

"Yes! It's there! What star is that?"

"Polaris. The pole star. The whole sky revolves around it."

"Wow! And that's really because we're rotating, right?"

"Right. And Polaris is the end of the handle of the Little Dipper. It's harder to see because its stars are fainter. It's about the same shape as the Big Dipper, but smaller and aimed the opposite way." Eric lifted lifted Marianne's hand until it pointed to one side of Polaris. "See it?"

Eric could almost feel the epiphany come upon Marianne. "I do! Wow! The Little Dipper! How do you *know* all this stuff?"

Eric released her hand and stood. "I read books. Lots of them. About lots of things."

In one rapid-fire lesson, Eric took Charlene and Marianne through the hallmarks of the late summer sky: Scorpius, the teapot of Sagittarius, the Summer Triangle, Delphinus, the Great Square of Pegasus, and all the bright stars from horizon to horizon. Halfway through the tour, he felt Charlene's soft, small fingers wriggle their way between his. He lost his train of thought, and caught himself wondering where Achernar was. No, wait—that wouldn't be visible this early until October. Only one thing was clear in his mind:

A beautiful girl was holding his hand.

"Please show me Lyra," Charlene asked. Eric's heart was pounding. "In the book I read, it actually looked like a harp."

Lyra was almost at the zenith. Eric craned his neck back until he felt it pop. "Straight up. A very bright white star with a touch of blue. That's Vega, Alpha Lyrae. It's one of the brightest stars in the sky. You can't miss it."

"Yes! It was so bright and beautiful in that book. I wanted a T-shirt with 'Lyra' on it, printed in gold ink on black above the constellation. I wanted it to be my symbol."

Eric pointed at Vega. "Lyra is a parallelogram, with Vega above and to the right of it. Four stars. It would be easier to see if it wasn't straight up."

"That's easy to fix," Charlene said, and sat on the sand. She stretched her legs out toward the water, and lay down. "I see it! Perfectly! It's better even than the book!"

"No picture of the stars ever does them justice." Eric pointed again, almost to the zenith. "To the right of Lyra is Hercules. It looks like a keystone."

Charlene grabbed Eric's ankle. "Don't look straight up like that. You'll hurt your neck. Lie down like me." She turned to her sister. "Marianne, you too."

"I dunno about this," Marianne grumbled, but complied.

Eric hesitated, looking back toward the trees that separated the beach from the tent sites. He had done plenty of observing flat on his back. It was certainly a more comfortable position for looking at the zenith. But he'd never done it with a girl—or anyone else—beside him.

Once Marianne was stretched out on the sand, he sat down between the two girls, took one more nervous glance toward the road and the trees, and lay down himself.

The lecture began again. He explained how you could follow the curve of the Big Dipper's handle and "arc to Arcturus," and later, following the same general curve, continue to Spica. He showed them the close pair of stars called the "cat's eyes" at the stinger end of Scorpius. Wistfully, he told them that if he had his telescope finished, he could show them the rings of Saturn.

Eric heard Charlene wriggling toward him on the crunchy sand. Her hand gripped his right arm. The next thing he knew, her head was on his shoulder, her body pressed against his side. He had the intuition that she was paying but a fraction of the rapt attention that she had shown only minutes before. His tour of the sky stopped abruptly.

A slow, silent minute ticked past. Eric oscillated between elation and dread.

Dread won, in the form of Marianne's agitated voice. "Hey, Shar, what are you doing over there? If mom sees us lying down like this, she'll be mad."

"Your mom is always mad."

"You're lying down and hugging a boy!"

Charlene looked over Eric's recumbent body at her sister "I'm hugging my friend."

"He's a boy. It's not like hugging mom."

Charlene's voice grew sharp. "Your mom hugs *you*. She's never hugged *me*. Ever. And your dad never hugs anybody. Who am *I* supposed to hug?"

The last thing Eric needed was for the girls to get in a screaming match across his ribcage. The pale green luminous hands of his watch showed 9:41. He had promised Mr. and Mrs. Sawyer to get their daughters back to the site before ten. This was as good an excuse as any.

"Um, we have to go home now. It's quarter to ten."

Eric helped Charlene to her feet, with Marianne standing nearby, her arms crossed. Charlene rubbed her eyes and cheeks against the sleeves of her T-shirt. Once their three flashlights were lit, they walked back to the tents without another word. Charlene's limp was still obvious, but she did not take Eric's arm. And one faint smile was her only reaction when he finally said 'G'night".

6

Eric's parents were at the site's picnic table, playing Monopoly under the Coleman lantern's light. Each had a plastic glass of wine, and his father's hand was over his mother's, as was often the case in quiet moments like these.

"I'll bet the girls learned something about astronomy," his mother said, smoothing Eric's hair and leaning away from the table to kiss his ear.

"Did you learn anything about girls?" his father asked, grinning.

"Jack, don't tease him." Marcia turned to Eric and pointed at the tent. "Z's. Now. Love you."

"Dream big," his father said.

As quietly as he could, Eric zipped down the big tent's mosquito-net door and pushed the canvas flap aside. The tent had three rooms: one for kids, one for grownups, and a central room piled with suitcases and cartons of sodas. Eric slipped under the canvas flap into the kids' room. He took off his shoes in near-silence, hoping not to disturb Lisa.

No luck. "Eric, I forgot to give you something."

Eric hunkered down beside his sister's sleeping bag. She pulled a little piece of paper folded in half from under her pillow and handed it to him.

"From Charlene."

Eric pulled his flashlight from his shorts pocket and unfolded the paper. It was just three lines, like a poem that didn't rhyme:

I said hi to you.

Your family welcomed me.

I'm a happy girl.

"You were out with your glider when she came by with it. Then mom took me to the playground and I forgot."

"Did you read it?"

"Yes." Lisa pulled the edge of her sleeping bag up over her head, giggling.

Eric smiled. "It's ok." He leaned over toward his own sleeping bag, and tucked the paper under his pillow.

Lisa was suddenly serious. "Do you love her?"

Eric stopped short. In response to his sister's question, he felt a pang of *something*—several somethings, all muddled together so thoroughly he couldn't put a name to any of them. "Leese, I just met her this morning. Dad told me love takes time, and not to hurry it."

"I heard mom tell Aunt Kate that the first time she met dad, she had instant chemistry with him. What's chemistry?"

He'd heard that story too. Within their family, Eric's parents were famously affectionate, and bragged about how lucky they were to have found each other. His father held his mother in very high regard. Eric realized that that was what he really wanted: to hold a girl in high regard, in the hopes that she would hold him in high regard in return. Was that love? Maybe, if it lasted long enough. He doubted it was chemistry.

"Chemistry means you like somebody really fast."

"So you and Charlene are having chemistry?"

Ulp. He should have seen *that* one coming. Eric powerfully suspected that chemistry in this context had something to do with sex, and sex was something he didn't really understand and didn't want to think about. His father had explained enough for him to be sure that sex was *not* what he wanted. What he wanted was hard to define, but all roads led back to that one idea: He wanted a girl to hold him in high regard.

"No. We're friends. It's possible to be friends right away—but it doesn't have to be chemistry-fast. And you should be doing some Z's too, shouldn't you?"

"I think she loves you."

"Leese!"

"G'night! I'm sleeping!" Lisa ducked down into her sleeping bag until all Eric could see was the top of her head. He laughed under his breath, and reached out to tousle her hair. Lisa had an uncanny knack for asking awkward questions. She could be annoying—but he suspected that he could be as well.

Eric wriggled into his sleeping bag, dirty socks and all. The campground had a shower building, no big deal. Tomorrow. He reached under his pillow and touched Charlene's poem. Something had happened. Charlene wasn't a happy girl anymore. Eric wasn't sure he had anything to do with that—but he wasn't sure that he didn't, either.

7

Eric was finishing up the breakfast dishes when his father came up behind him and rested his hand on his son's shoulder. "Hey, chief."

Eric looked down at his shoulder. In his father's hand was a five-dollar bill.

"Take her down to the campground store and buy her an ice-cream cone."

"Lisa?"

Jack thumped his son's shoulder. "Don't play dense. Charlene."

"That doesn't cost five dollars."

"Give the five to the man at the store while she's watching, and put the change in your pocket. Make sure Charlene knows she's special."

"Dad, I just met her yesterday." Eric put a Melmac bowl down on the stack.

"The day I met your mother, I asked her to go down the street and have a pizza with me. Sparks flew."

"I don't want sparks."

Jack stuffed the five-spot in his son's back pocket. "That's good. Sparks are for when you're 19. In the meantime, be a friend. A good friend."

"That doesn't take ice cream."

His father shrugged. "Maybe not. But it sure as hell won't hurt!"

8

Eric found Charlene standing on the beach at the edge of the water, staring out across the lake, a light breeze stirring her chestnut-brown hair. He stood on the road for a long minute, watching her. She didn't move. He crossed the sand to stand beside her. "I got your poem last night. Lisa gave it to me. Thank you."

Charlene turned and looked at him. "It's a haiku. They pop into my head and I write them down. It's weird how that happens. This one was about your parents."

"My parents?"

"It's wonderful the way they show how they love each other, right out in the open. I wonder sometimes if my parents even *like* each other. Your parents' love spills out all over everything, including you and Lisa—and yesterday, even me."

Tears began their slow path down Charlene's cheeks. Eric felt a pang of regret. Somehow this had to be his fault. "You're crying. Did...I hurt you somehow?"

Charlene shook her head. She reached out her pinky finger and touched his hand for just a moment. "How could you? When my head was on your shoulder last night, I felt like I *belonged* there. And then my sister had to mess it up." She wiped her eyes on her sleeve. "I don't belong anywhere."

"That's not true."

"So where do I belong?"

There was a pain in her voice that frightened Eric. His mouth opened, but nothing would come together in words that might comfort her. The obvious sounded banal to him, but it was the best he could do. "Here. Where you are."

"You mean with you."

"With me. Or with anyone else. Or with no one at all." Eric remembered something whimsical that Aunt Kate had told him back when he was staying with her family while Lisa was being born, and he was feeling homesick. He adapted it for the current moment. "There's a Charlene-shaped hole in the world, and only you can fill it."

She laughed. Her little finger touched the back of his hand and followed it to the end of his little finger, and then gripped his pinky with hers. "We should take a walk. I owe you an explanation."

"An explanation of what?"

"Lots of things." Charlene smiled for the first time. "Walk with me." She took his hand and began to walk toward the road.

Eric looked down at their clasped hands. "What if your mom sees us?"

Charlene looked away from him. "Last night I told mom I was going to hold hands with you, and if she didn't like it, she could throw me out on the street."

Eric was incredulous. "You said that to your mother?"

Charlene wasn't limping anymore. "She's not my mother."

It took awhile for Charlene to open up. Eric steered them in the direction of the campground entrance and store, mentioning casually that he intended to buy her an ice-cream cone. Perhaps thinking that he was trying to change the subject, Charlene began.

"I have a cousin outside Chicago somewhere. When Sarah was fifteen, she got pregnant. That was thirteen years ago."

Charlene didn't have to spell it out. Eric understood—maybe. "You mean, your cousin is your real mother."

"Yes. She wanted to raise me. Her parents were already divorced. My grandmother was working two jobs to support herself and Sarah. My great-grandparents were furious. They told Sarah to give me up for adoption. There was a huge fight. My stepdad offered to adopt me. Claire wanted no part of it. My stepdad browbeat her into it. So they adopted me anyway.

"It wasn't until last year that they told me the whole story. It broke my heart. My real mom didn't want to give me up, and my stepmom didn't want to take me. I've seen Sarah twice—at my great-grandparents' funerals down in Chicago—and she wouldn't even talk to me." Charlene sniffled, and wiped her eyes on her sleeve.

"So who is your real father?"

"Nobody will tell me. I'm sure it was just some boy Sarah knew. 'Things got out of control,' as Claire puts it. She keeps warning me about boys. My sister and I go to school at home. Where would I meet boys? I don't have any friends. I certainly don't have any friends who are boys. I like my cousin Linda in Beloit a lot. My aunt and uncle are really nice. Mom lets me spend weekends there just to get rid of me."

Having met Claire Sawyer, Eric could not say he didn't believe it. "Linda's a friend."

Charlene blushed. "Yes. She is. Linda's already fifteen but she treats me like I'm her age. When I was there two weeks ago, she had three of her friends to her house for a sleepover. They treated me like I was one of them. They taught me how to put nail polish on my toes." Charlene glanced down at her feet, now in battered tennis shoes. "It looked so weird, seeing my toes all bright red. But their toes were red too. I felt like I belonged to them."

Eric nodded. "So that's why I wrapped your little toe in a bandaid."

"Yes. Before my dad came to pick me up, I had Linda take off the polish. I asked her to leave the color on one toe, so I could remember what it felt like to belong to them."

For several minutes neither Eric nor Charlene spoke. On both sides of the road were families, sharing meals, playing cards, laughing, having fun being together. To Eric, that was just how life worked. It was hard for him to imagine how life would be without it. Yet that was Charlene's life.

Suddenly, an ice-cream cone seemed like an awfully small thing to offer her.

"Eric, I got mad at mom yesterday at dinner for asking you stupid personal questions. I'm not going to excuse her. But you need to understand that she's terrified of some boy making me pregnant like some boy made my real mom pregnant, so that the whole thing will start all over again. It's really strange because I just turned 12 in April. I don't know any boys. And I'm not that dumb. But that's all she thinks about."

"Um, I promise never to make you pregnant."

Charlene laughed, released Eric's hand, slapped it lightly, and clasped it again. "Wrong promise. I want you to promise me that you'll always want the best for me—and that I get to decide what 'the best' is."

"Well, sure. Solemn promise. Isn't that how friendship works?"

"It is. But some people get things all mixed up. Like my real mother—both mothers, actually, though not the same things. I don't think my real mother wanted to get pregnant. But she wanted to belong to somebody. She had no father and was growing up poor and mostly alone. I don't think Claire wanted kids at all. Not even my sister. In both cases, dad talked her into it."

"Um, was that a good idea?"

Charlene shrugged. "I had to go somewhere. My grandmother and Sarah were poor. Dad makes a good living. So maybe it was a bad idea that had to happen to make things less bad overall, if that makes any sense."

"I guess. I just wish you didn't have to be hurt by—"

Charlene let go of his hand, put her hand around Eric's waist, and pulled him close to her. "If you start thinking that any of this is your fault, I'll hit you."

"I'm sure just being with me didn't help—"

Charlene took her hand from his waist, made a fist, and hit his shoulder, hard.

"Oww! You don't pull punches, do you?" Eric rubbed his shoulder and grimaced at Charlene.

"No. I lift my dad's weights." Charlene took his hand again. "If I ever tell you I'm going to hit you, *believe* it!"

"Ok. I give. None of this is my fault." Eric always tried not to lie. But if he wasn't sure none of it was his fault…was it still a lie?

9

Across a breezeway from the campground office was a little red barn in the shape of a big red barn. A battered ice freezer stood to the right of the front door, and bags of charcoal were lined up across the width of the barn's rough wood porch. For sale inside were most of the things a family might need for a week's camping: apples, beach balls, frozen hamburgers, all kinds of canned food (including, Eric noticed instantly, Dinty Moore Beef Stew) milk, rolls, butter, dog food, kites, and at the far end of the room, an ice-cream counter with eight different flavors and three kinds of cones.

There was a line. Charlene stared through the glass at the ice cream cartons while they waited for the kids in front of them to buy their cones. "My folks don't let us have ice cream very often. Maybe Christmas. And birthdays. So what's 'French Silk'? I love chocolate ice cream."

Eric knew, from some idle time and money spent at Baskin Robbins on Arlington Heights Road. "It's milk-chocolate ice cream with milk-chocolate chips."

"Ooooh, I *have* to have that! And Eric, please, may I have two scoops?"

"Anything for—" Eric caught himself; was he really about to say "my girlfriend?" She was holding his hand and leaning against his shoulder. If she wasn't his girlfriend, what was she?

She was Charlene. And that was special all by itself.

"—for you."

They left the campground store with sugar cones of French silk ice cream; Charlene with two scoops and Eric with one. Behind the store was a grassy area with picnic tables where a lot of middle schoolers and young teens stood around, sitting at or leaning on the tables, eating their ice cream and talking.

They found an empty table and leaned against one end. Charlene caught a chocolate drip with her tongue before it left her cone. "I saw most of these kids last summer. It's wild how many people come here year after year."

"I can see why. It's a great place. I can't wait to come back with my telescope."

Charlene's expression changed to something halfway between fear and exultation. "Do you think your folks will bring you back next year?"

Eric gripped her free hand and squeezed it. "Sure. Especially if you'll be here. My dad really likes you."

"Wow! He's wonderful! And Lisa is *so* cute. So…a lick for luck?"

"Um, *what?*"

She laughed. "We both make a wish. Then you lick my cone and I'll lick yours. It's like a kiss for luck without the kiss. If it all works out, both our wishes will come true."

"Do you have a wish?"

"I sure do! So make a wish already!"

Eric could only think of a single wish worth wishing: That he would see Charlene again someday after their family campouts were over.

"Done."

She tilted her ice cream cone forward, right under Eric's lips. He took a long lick. He didn't remember ever enjoying French Silk ice cream as much as he did at that moment. He then lifted his cone and held it before her lips. Her tongue darted out, lingered over the cone for a moment, and withdrew.

"We're going to get our wishes," she said, with a certainty that Eric longed to feel as well.

"I hope so."

"I *know* so."

They leaned back against the table, taking occasional licks from their cones, reveling in one another's presence. There was a clot of kids about their age, laughing and poking each other two tables over. Charlene pointed out those she knew from previous years at Castle Rock Lake. Some waved to her, and she waved back.

"They think you're my boyfriend," Charlene said. She reached her left arm around Eric's waist and pulled him close to her. She crept her hand up from his waist to his upper arm, and gripped his biceps.

Eric waved at the girls. "I'm good with that."

Charlene tipped her head until it touched Eric's shoulder. "So am I."

There was a boy in the group the next table over, laughing and getting a little too close to the girls. Eric couldn't quite make out what he was saying, but one by one he was leaning in to kiss them. A few of the girls turned their faces away in embarrassment. Some seemed more than willing to play whatever stupid game he was playing.

"That's Randy," Charlene said. She lowered her voice. "He's a weasel."

"Looks like it."

"I had to tell him to get lost last year." She took another lick from her cone. "I don't do that stuff."

Eric said nothing.

Randy ambled over to stand in front of them. "Hey, Charlene. Boyfriend or bodyguard?"

Charlene rolled her eyes. "The magic word is 'and'."

"You owe me a kiss from last year."

"Get lost."

Eric pushed away from the table and straightened. Randy looked Eric in the eye. "Bodyguard, huh? Do you think you can take me?"

Eric idly scratched his nose. "To the dump? Sure." The boy was several inches shorter than he, with tight blond curls and ruddy skin scattered with freckles. The eyes riveted on Eric's were pale blue.

The two boys glared at each other. Eric's father had spent time advising his unconventional son how to deal with boys like Randy: *When you're beset by a bully, stand firm.*

Randy knocked the ice-cream cone from Eric's hand. It splattered to the grass. Eric kept eye contact, and leaned forward. He saw the tension in Randy's face. "You made a mess. You can leave now."

"I'll leave when I get what I want." Randy grasped Charlene's arm. "You could do worse than kiss me," he said, at less than arm's length from her face.

"I guess I could eat rat poison." She tried to shake his hand free, but Randy wouldn't release her.

Eric had had enough. He took a half-step toward Randy. "Let her go."

Randy released Charlene's arm and pushed her roughly to one side. "I don't take orders from beanpoles like you."

"You just did."

Randy swung his fist at Eric's face. The movement was clumsy and none too fast. Eric caught Randy's forearm and held it like a vice. Randy's voice was thick with tension—and beneath it, what Eric knew was fear. "I can kiss her if I want to, and I don't care what anybody thinks!"

Never losing eye contact, Eric tightened his grip on Randy's arm and started to twist.

"Leggo of me!"

Eric continued to twist. His father's lesson had worked well. Randy began to lean in the direction of the twist, clearly in discomfort.

"Leggo!"

With a downward shove, Eric released Randy's arm. Randy stumbled to his knees, then rose, and staggered toward Charlene.

With a movement like a wood beam in a tornado, Charlene spun and kicked Randy in the crotch. The boy fell to the ground, curled up on himself, squelching what Eric knew were agonized cries.

Charlene stood over him and spoke slowly, her voice more forceful than Eric had ever heard it. "Go home, Randy. If you ever touch me again, Eric and I will both beat the living shit out of you."

Randy got to his knees, shook his head, and with some clumsiness got to his feet. He limped down the road without speaking or looking back.

Eric and Charlene took their time walking back to their family tents. "Ok. That was close," she said. "What if he'd tried to fight you?"

"I would have fought back. He was nervous and just trying to save face by swinging at me. I would have grabbed both his arms and kicked his legs out from under him. Or, if I had the chance, I'd probably do what you did. Where'd you learn that, anyway?"

Charlene laughed. "Mom taught me, using Dad's big punching bag that hangs from a beam in the basement. She wanted me to know how to defend myself from scum like Randy."

"She's a good teacher. Then there's how you told him what we would do to him if he touched you again. That was pretty impressive. Who taught you that?"

Charlene grinned. "Same answer."

10

Eric ate lunch with Charlene's family at their campground table, in their usual silence. He sensed tension in the air, and was relieved when Mr. and Mrs. Sawyer told them they were going for a walk. He and Charlene watched them set off down the campground road. Eric knew that if it were his parents they would be holding hands, bumping shoulders now and then, laughing or even singing together softly, in harmony.

No. The Sawyers kept three feet between them at all times.

"They're mad," Marianne said, joining them at their picnic table.

Charlene nodded. "I got snotty with mom last night. I'm sure she's complaining to dad."

"They used to like each other," Marianne said. "I miss that."

"Me too." Charlene opened her little pocket spiral notebook to a blank page. She doodled what looked like Yogi Bear. "Eric, why do you like me so much?"

Eric swallowed hard and leaned back, startled. It was not a question he had expected. "Why wouldn't I?"

"Stop dodging." She began a sketch of Eric's nonplused face on her notebook.

Eric looked over his shoulder to see if the Sawyers were out of sight, and then, sure he wouldn't be seen, placed his hand over Charlene's. "Because you speak in complete sentences."

Charlene laughed, and brushed his hand away. "Don't interrupt me when I'm drawing." She put her pencil back to her little notebook. "Words and pictures are what I am."

When the drawing was complete a minute or two later, Eric felt that it captured his mood perfectly. "My mom pointed it out five minutes after I met you. She's an English teacher. She appreciates that sort of thing. And so do I."

Another few pencil strokes, and the sketch was finished. "You always speak in complete sentences too. I don't have a monopoly on that."

Eric sighed. "The girls at my school laugh at me when I talk. It's not like I'm putting on airs. I just want to be understood. And the harder I try, the more they laugh at me."

"They're idiots," Marianne said, frowning, slamming one palm with her fist.

"No." Eric looked down in his lap. "It's nervous laughter. I'm so different they don't know how to deal with me. So they don't." He managed a grin. "I'm good with that."

"Me too," Charlene said in something close to a whisper.

Marianne drummed her fingers on the table. "Hey, I'm sorry I busted up your hug last night." She looked at Charlene. "Mom's been really grouchy lately. I was afraid she'd come down to the beach and yell at us." Marianne was silent for long seconds, but Eric could tell she wasn't finished. "She told me once, 'girls don't get pregnant standing up.' I didn't want to get that lecture every day again for the next three weeks." She turned to Eric. "And thank you for helping me find the constellations. I'll never look at the stars the same way again."

"I won't either." Charlene started writing on her notebook page below her sketch of Eric. She tore off the sheet and handed it to him. It was another poem:

Complete sentences
Are the language we both speak
That binds us as friends.

"Yes," Eric said. "Exactly that." He casually turned the sheet over. There was another poem on the other side:

> We'll be leaving soon.
> How will I live without him?
> One day at a time.

Charlene's eyes widened. "Hey, that wasn't for you!"

"You handed it to me." He offered Charlene the small sheet of paper with ragged perforations at the top.

She waved it back. "Ok, it's yours."

"No. Change 'him' to 'her,' and *then* it's mine."

11

Eric had promised to take Lisa down to the beach at the warmest part of the day. So at 2:30 he took her hand and started off down the road, she in little bunny sandals and her swimsuit with the short ruffled skirt, he in his trunks, barefoot, a T-shirt wadded up in his hand and two towels clamped in his armpit.

He was not surprised to see Charlene and Marianne already there. Marianne was at the waterline, picking up small stones and throwing them into the lake. Charlene was sitting cross-legged on the sand a little way up from the water, with a bucket beside her, and a couple of battered tin cups and a butterknife beside the bucket. Unlike Marianne, she was dressed in the same shorts and T-shirt she had worn at lunch. She still wore her tennis shoes, which spoke volumes without words. Eric ached for her.

Charlene was shaping a mound of sand in front of her, sometimes dipping water out of the bucket, sometimes sifting sand between her fingers onto the mound, or running the butterknife in graceful strokes across parts of her sculpture.

As Eric drew up beside her, he saw that she was sculpting a cartoon bear dancing atop a ball. Lisa was entranced. "Wow! That's a good bear!"

"Thanks, Lisa. It's turning out pretty much as I envisioned it."

"You really are an artist!"

Charlene bowed at the waist, laughing. "And you're the best audience any artist could want!"

Lisa turned toward her brother. "Eric, I want to go in the water."

Eric pointed at the lake. "Let's go, then!" He took his little sister's hand and ran into the water. She jumped across the waterline into ankle-depth water, and sat down. "I love this lake!" She looked up at Eric. "I love you too!"

"Likewise, Leese." He squeezed her hand and let it go.

Marianne trotted over, a beach ball under one arm and a stone in her other hand. "Hey, Eric. I've been trying to skip a stone all afternoon. Is it a boy thing?"

"No. It's a practice thing." Eric held out his hand. Marianne dropped the stone on his palm. "This one's a little too thick. You really want the flattest stone you can find." Eric kicked up some stones from the sand, bent down to pick one up, and handed it to her. "Flat. Now hold it with your thumb and forefinger, resting the flat side on your middle finger." He picked up another stone and held it as he had described. "Like this."

Marianne positioned the stone in her fingers. Eric nodded in approval. "Good. Now watch me. The idea is to spin it when you throw it, and send it forward so that the flat face hits the water. If it hits just right, it'll bounce off the water, go a little ways more, hit the water, and bounce again."

Eric stretched his arm back, and spun the stone horizontally across the water. It struck the surface four times before sinking out of sight.

Marianne's eyes grew wide. "Four skips! I'd be happy with one! How'd you learn to do that?"

Eric shrugged. He spotted four or five more flat stones and fished them out of the sand. "I had to pick up a lot of stones. My arm got sore. Eventually I got it right."

Marianne laughed as Eric handed the stones to her. She slipped the stones into a pocket. She held the stone Eric had given her as he demonstrated, and sent it spinning over the quiet lake. The stone skipped not once but twice before sinking.

"I did it! I did it!" She spun around, laughing. "Twice! Can I have a boyfriend like you someday? I mean, one who can explain everything to me and make it look easy? He wouldn't have to get all mushy with me."

"Look for the boys that the other girls laugh at," Eric said.

"You mean, the ones who talk in complete sentences."

"Yup. They're out there. Watch for them."

Marianne bounced the beach ball against the sand. "Hey. I'll play catch with Lisa so you can go talk to Charlene. She's been acting sad since lunch. I think she needs you."

"Thanks. I will."

Eric walked the few yards up the beach to where Charlene continued to work on her bear. She patted the sand into place, sculpting it with her fingers and occasionally grabbing more wet sand from the bucket.

"Wow, that's cool!" Eric said. "How did you learn to do that?"

Charlene set a tin cup half-full of wet sand down beside her. "I don't know. I just do it. I like bears. I see a bear in my head, and then I draw one with sand. That's one reason I like this campground. The lake has good sand. Dad says they trucked it all in to make a beach, like that was a bad thing. Lake Michigan has good sand, but the water is *really* cold." She smoothed the bear's tummy with three fingers, then looked out toward the water, where Lisa was bouncing the ball across the sand to Marianne. "I watched you teach my sister how to skip stones. Boy, if she didn't have a crush on you before, she has one now."

Eric laughed a little. "She said she wants a boyfriend like me someday. I wonder if she understands what she's wishing for."

"If she doesn't, I'll explain it to her. Just taking her seriously like you do means more to her than you think. Mom treats her like a five-year-old. The way you showed us the constellations last night, that was just *amazing*." Charlene reached out to touch up the bear's big feet with the butterknife. "Do you think of me as your girlfriend?"

Eric twitched. Charlene had a way of asking unexpected questions. There was an obvious answer, and a subtler one. "You're my friend. You're a girl. Does that answer the question?"

"No. You're dodging again." She looked up at him, her eyes sparkling. "What does 'girlfriend' mean to you?"

Time for the subtler answer, which (as usual) was probably the truer one. "A girlfriend is a girl whom you hold in high regard. It sounds silly, but my mother is my father's wife, but she's also his girlfriend."

Charlene gazed off toward the trees, looking wistful. "I hope she's always his girlfriend."

"Me too—though having known them all my life, I'd bet on it. And…there's the other half: A girlfriend is a girl who holds you in high regard back. Um, that's what I want in a girlfriend."

"Do you hold me in high regard?"

Eric again felt deep stirrings that he couldn't name. "Yes. Yes, I do."

"Then I'm your girlfriend."

"So you—"

"Hold you in high regard? How could I not? You're the smartest boy I've ever met. You're always polite and willing to help. Even mom admits you've been raised right. She says that boys who respect their elders will respect me as well."

"That's a rule at our house."

"I can tell. So, yes. I hold you in high regard. I never thought of it in those words, but if I ever had a boyfriend, that's exactly what I would want from him. And…now I have a boyfriend."

Charlene reached out and put her hand over his. Eric put his other hand over hers. "That simple, huh?" he said.

"Yes. Now shush." She touched his lips with one finger. Eric nodded, and finally understood that whatever was happening, he would never be the same.

12

Eric's father liked pizza a lot. He liked baseball even more. The Cubs were playing game two of a three-game series against the Giants. So at 6:30 the Lunds piled into the Impala and drove to the Wagonwheel Grill in downtown Mauston. Once their family-size pizza arrived, Jack took a slice on a paper napkin and went to the bar, where the game was up on a color TV.

Eric was quiet. He had wanted to ask Charlene what was wrong, but she wasn't having it. The impossible had happened: She now claimed that he was her boyfriend, and she was his girlfriend. Beyond that she didn't want to talk. Eric had watched her sculpt her bear in silence for another twenty minutes before wandering back to the water to play three-corner catch with Lisa and Marianne.

Being a boyfriend was evidently a trickier business than he had imagined.

His mother had cut Lisa's slice in half, and was coaching her on how to get it into her mouth without smearing tomato sauce in her clothes and hair. Eric stared into a corner of the crowded grill, where there was a wall-mounted lamp in the shape of the Hamm's bear. He was sure Charlene would like to have something like that. Even if he could find one—and afford it—would the Sawyers appreciate the gift of a beer company ad to their daughter? The frightening thing was that Eric just couldn't tell.

"Hey, #1 son. You're being awfully quiet. Thinking about Charlene?"

Eric heaved a sigh. "Mom, c'mon. I've never had a girl like me before. I'm trying to figure it out."

His mother leaned over and kissed the side of his head above one ear. "She's a very forthright girl. She saw you and knew she had to have you. And why not? You're smart, polite, and good-looking."

"Mom—"

"You think I'm kidding? I'm not."

"I think Charlene loves him," Lisa said, her mouth half-full of pizza.

"That might be stretching it." Eric didn't want to sound sharp to his little sister. He was in a very unsettled mood, and couldn't clearly see why. He had a girlfriend! But two days ago, he didn't even know that he wanted one. Or did he?

"Love doesn't happen in two days." Marcia took a long sip from her wine glass.

Lisa tilted her head. "Mom, how long was it before you loved dad? Was it more than two days?"

The bar waitress came by. Marcia Lund drained her glass of wine and ordered another. "Oh, yes. When I met him, your father was larger than life. He was almost a foot taller than I was, and solid muscle. He scared the hell out of me at first. I had this sense that he had chosen me and would not take 'no' for an answer."

"I'd choose you too," Lisa said. "You're the best mom *ever*."

Marcia kissed her finger, and pressed it against Lisa's cheek. "Thanks, baby. I need to hear that now and then." She looked back toward Eric. "I was nervous. But he was funny, and courteous, and could talk about anything. He drew me into conversation. It was uncanny. He could get me to talk about all my crazy dreams, and he did his best to encourage me. He *listened* to me. Nobody had ever listened to me that intently before. He never demanded that I avoid the other boys at school. I dated a few of them. They were…ordinary. It was like they were in black and white, and my Jack was in Technicolor and Cinemascope. There came a day when I realized that I couldn't live without him. I told him I loved him. He told me he loved me too. He was 21 and I was 19. I'd known him for six months."

Eric saw the glisten of moisture in his mother's eyes. "Mom, what's wrong?"

She grinned, wiped her eyes on a paper napkin, and patted his shoulder. "My little boy is growing up." She took another sip of wine. "And I just had this strange insight that someday, some girl will be telling this same story to her children—about you."

"Me."

"Yes, you. You're *so* much like your father. Someday, some girl will realize that she just can't live without you. It won't be Charlene—but it'll be somebody."

Over in the bar, men were cheering. Eric figured that Ernie Banks had knocked another one out of the park. He was thinking about Charlene's poem—the one she had not intended for him to see.

Yes. Love took more than two days. And maybe it took a *lot* more than two days. The notion of being twenty-one was completely beyond him. That would be 1975. We'd be on the Moon! There would be flying cars! Maybe. With luck. And would someone be there beside him, like his mother had been beside his father?

It was almost easier to imagine being on the Moon.

It won't be Charlene—but it'll be somebody.

Did the choice *have* to be that stark?

13

Eric had slept badly. The haze of a restless night lingered over his thoughts all through breakfast. His parents still considered him too young to have coffee, though this was the sort of morning he would have liked to try it. Lack of sleep had made him tense and grumpy. While he washed the breakfast dishes Lisa had asked him again if he loved Charlene. His snapped "No!" made her cry. His father told him sternly to take a walk. His mother suggested the campground store, to bring back a salami for sandwiches and a bag of marshmallows, adding that they were going to take Lisa to the beach.

The walk and the errand helped only a little. The haze retreated, to be replaced by now-constant desire to be with Charlene. He wanted to talk to her, and feel her hand holding his. The memory of her pressed up against him on the beach was vivid, spawning fantasies of cuddling and comforting her. Eric caught himself imagining pulling her hated shoes off so she could be barefoot again.

His thoughts kept returning to the beach at night beneath exuberant stars. Just a few minutes more was all he wanted, lying side-by-side with Charlene on the sand…and then Marianne had to go and ruin it.

Sisters!

So what was really going on? All Charlene had been doing was hugging him. Was that so bad? His mother hugged him. Lisa hugged him. Aunt Kate and his cousin Mary Catherine hugged him. It was a warm and comfortable feeling.

No. This was different. *Completely* different.

It frightened him a little to ponder how different it was.

Eric pulled another marshmallow out of the torn-open bag. He had already eaten four. If he didn't stop, he'd have to buy another bag with his own money. The fifth marshmallow was down the hatch when Charlene came running across the field.

From a long way off, Eric could see that something was terribly wrong. He had seen her sad, thoughtful, and jubilant. This was something else, something much darker.

She came up to him and grasped his right hand. "Eric, Eric, I need to talk to you. Alone."

"Ok." He stopped, and glanced around. "I guess we're alone."

Charlene pulled on his arm. "No. I want us to be alone, and where no one can see us." She pointed to a garage beside the campground office. "Let's go over behind that building."

They walked through the grass across the field, to where the trees began again. In the half-light beneath the pines and in the shadow of the campground's garage, Charlene stopped and faced Eric.

"Something awful happened last night. Mom and dad had a horrible fight, right in front of my sister and me. Dad is packing up the tent and everything. As soon as he's done, we're leaving."

He felt her words like a kick to the gut. "What happened?"

Charlene shook her head. "I don't want to talk about it. I'll tell you someday. I hope. If…Eric, hold me. Please hold me."

Eric had no idea what to say. He held out his arms to her.

Charlene threw her arms around him and buried her face in his shoulder. "It's all coming apart. Dad used the word 'divorce.' Mom hit him and called him all kinds of names. I'm scared. Marianne and I were in the corner of the tent while it all went on. But that's not the worst part. I learned who my real father is."

"Who?"

"I can't tell you. It's horrible! Just hold me. Please!"

For several very long minutes, the only sound was Charlene sobbing into Eric's shoulder. What could he say that would comfort her?

"Charlene, I…um…I…"

She reached up and put her index finger against his lips. "Please don't tell me you love me. That's not what I want from you. I keep thinking I know what love is—and then I keep realizing I'm wrong. My folks supposedly love me. They even say so once in a while. Then there was last night." Charlene sniffled. "The word 'love' means so many things that I wonder sometimes if it means anything at all."

She pushed away from Eric a little. "I always assumed we'd be back next year, but now I don't know. I may never see you again. I've never felt what I'm feeling for you for anybody before. I don't know what to think." She looked into Eric's eyes with an expression he could only think of as torment. "Except that I want you to be my first."

Eric felt a strange buzz in the roof of his mouth. "Your first *what?*"

"This." Charlene reached up and put both hands behind Eric's neck, and pulled his head down toward hers. Her lips met his, lingered for a moment, and parted. "Nothing will ever change what we have together. No matter what happens to me. Nothing."

With that she turned and ran back across the field to her family's campsite.

Eric was crushed. Head down, he continued across the field. By the time he reached his own campsite, five more marshmallows were gone. Lisa and his parents were still at the beach. Eric could no longer hear the busy sounds of camp being broken at the next site. He assumed Charlene's family was ready to leave the campground.

Eric sat alone at the picnic table. A short pile of books was by his side. He could not force himself to be interested in them. Between his elbows lay his planisphere. Were it not for that odd little piece of cardboard, he might never have met her. Or—he might have met her, but might not have recognized who and what she was: a girl who saw the world as he did.

A girl who spoke in complete sentences.

Eric put his head in his hands.

D id you really think I'd leave without saying goodbye?"
Eric looked up. Charlene stood beside him, a wan smile on her face and a sketchpad in her hands.

"How did you sneak up on me like that?"

She pointed downward. Charlene was barefoot. And—she had removed the Band-Aid from her little toe, its bright red polish a brilliant gem in the subdued forest light. "I'm tired of hiding. If mom doesn't like it, it's not my problem anymore."

Eric stood and faced her. This was a species of bravery he hoped he could find someday if he ever needed it. "I'll pray for you."

She bowed her head. "Thank you. No. *Dziękuję*."

"*Nie ma za co.*"

Charlene placed the sketchpad on both her hands and extended them toward him.

Eric took the sketchpad and began to open it. Charlene placed a hand over his. "Don't open it now. I'll cry."

"You've been crying a lot."

"I'll cry more. Open it later. But if you ever start thinking you just imagined me, open it again."

Eric turned to the picnic table and picked up his planisphere. "Please take this. If I can't be there to show you the stars, it'll give you a head start." He added quickly, "Um, there's instructions on the back."

Charlene scrunched up her face at him. They both broke into quiet laughter. He took her hands. "Thanks for everything."

"*Nie ma za co.*" Close by, a car started its engine. Charlene looked over her shoulder. "That's our Plymouth." She put her arms around him. "Thanks for belonging me."

"Belonging you?"

"For making me feel like I belong. When I'm with you I feel like I'm *home.*"

Eric looked down. This was it, then. What more could he say? "God be with you. That's what 'goodbye' means."

She looked into his eyes. "God *is* with me. I just never knew it until now. God be with you too."

The Plymouth's horn honked.

"Maybe you should go. They'll be mad."

Charlene touched her forehead to his shoulder. "They're already mad." She stood on tiptoe and pressed her lips against his for a moment. "I don't care."

A car stopped on the road. Its window rolled down. Mrs. Sawyer's shrill voice followed. "Charlene, stop that, and get over here!"

Charlene again looked over her shoulder. She turned back to Eric, and pressed her lips against his, harder, lingering for what Eric thought might be the longest seconds in his young life.

She pulled back. "I hold you in high regard."

Eric took both her hands one last time. "I hold you in high regard too."

Charlene let his hands go and took two steps backward, Eric's planisphere clamped under her arm, new tears on her cheeks. "Write to me!" She turned and ran to the car on the road. Eric closed his eyes. He heard the door slam. The car purred off down the campground road until birdsong and the laughter of the other campers rose over it.

Eric sat down at the picnic table. He turned the sketchpad cover over. Beneath it was a pencil drawing of a boy and a girl holding hands beneath a spectacularly starry sky. He flipped the page up before he had tears himself. On the following page was an address in Janesville, Wisconsin. He flipped the page again. In very decorative longhand, she had written:

> You showed me the stars.
> Your hand taught my hand this truth:
> I belong to you.

14

Trick or treat, Mr. Linksweiler!" Lisa shouted when the white-haired old man opened the door. He stood a little crookedly, but with his indomitable smile, few people noticed. According to Eric's father, Mr. Linksweiler was a brave man, an Army officer, and had won medals for his bravery. He had always put his men's lives ahead of his own. One of his legs was artificial, to replace the one that had been blown off in the last days of World War 1. Mr. Linksweiler liked to say, "God put it in the freezer, and told me He'd stick it back on once I got up there."

"I've got something special for you, Lady Lisa!" He turned away for a moment, and turned back with a little stuffed hedgehog in his hand. "When you feel lonely, just put him in both hands and ask God to send an angel for you to talk to. That's what I do."

Lisa took the toy in both hands and held it close to her heart. "Thank you, Mr. Linksweiler! I will!"

"And if all the angels are busy, a little chocolate won't hurt!" He dropped a handful of small chocolate bars into her bag. "You too, Master Lund. If you ever meet a lonely girl, give her chocolate. That's how I won my Angie, and loved her for sixty-six years." Mr. Linksweiler gave Eric a slightly larger handful of chocolate bars. Eric dropped them in his own bag, for a moment feeling a little silly dressed up as a pirate while begging candy from the neighbors.

What was happening to him?

"Thank you, sir. I will. Promise."

The old man waved at the two of them. "Happy Halloween. Guard Lady Lisa from monsters, Master Lund."

Eric bowed his head, his doubts abruptly gone, feeling like he was being knighted by a king. He drew his cardboard scimitar. "That's my job, Lieutenant Linksweiler!"

The old man saluted him. Eric saluted back. Mr. Linksweiler, still smiling, swung his door closed.

Lisa and Eric went down Mr. Linksweiler's front walk and took the last few yards to their house. The Sun was setting. It was quarter to six, and supper was at six-thirty. Lisa had been around several blocks with Eric. By the way she held her bag, he could tell she was getting tired. Their father, still in his business suit, opened the big front door and bent down so Lisa could hug him.

"Welcome home, Princess and Pirate! Dinner's in the works!"

Lisa ran into the kitchen. Eric set his bag down beside the door, his eyes settling on the pile of mail on the little telephone table, next to the basket of candy bars for the other neighborhood kids.

His father shook his head a little sadly. "No letters today, chief."

Eric and his father stood, still not quite face-to-face, but getting there as the months passed and the growth spurts happened. "Dad, what am I doing wrong?"

Jack Lund pointed at the livingroom couch. Eric sat, wondering what expression was on his face. His father took the place beside him. "My guess is…nothing."

"I've sent her six letters since August. I asked her how she was doing, what she was learning, if she liked the Monkees, what she thought of *Star Trek*." He paused, wondering how much of his private pourings-out he needed to mention.

"And no reply." His father leaned back and put one arm along the back of the couch. "She may be afraid."

"Of me?"

"No. She may be afraid of getting ahead of the game. She's home now. So are you. You're both back in ordinary life. Vacation is like having a second life where anything is possible. Back home, well, is home. Things work in familiar ways within familiar limits, and maybe she realized that being twelve is too soon to fall in love."

Eric's eyes met his father's. "Wait. Hold on. I never told her I loved her. She didn't say it to me either. I just want us to be friends. Really."

"Fair. And good common sense. But maybe she's so lonely that it hurts too much to even send you letters."

That hadn't occurred to Eric, but it was all too possible. He had never told his parents of the still-unexplained rupture of Charlene's family.

"So what do I do?"

Jack Lund leaned toward his son. "Stop writing to her. It may be hurting her to realize she'll never see you again. You don't want to hurt her."

The notion that his cheerful letters had caused Charlene pain chilled him. "I don't."

"Sometimes things just don't work out, as much as we want them to. Maybe it's better if you two think of each other as memories, rather than friends."

Eric looked down at the livingroom carpet. "I suppose."

"Someday it'll work out with someone."

"I hope so."

"It will. Hey, come on, you're twelve. You have everything you need to make friendship work, including time. *Especially* time. And hell, you're my son. Lunds don't lose. Keep trying."

Eric tried to smile, and mostly failed. He *had* been trying, trying as hard as he could. Still, before he even knew what to call the feelings he had for Charlene, Charlene was gone.

His father stood. "You didn't get any letters today, but the UPS man came, and brought something with your name on it."

Eric looked up, his mouth hanging open. "What?"

Jack Lund shrugged. "It's addressed to you. I don't open your mail." He pointed into the dining room. "Let's take a look."

Eric followed his father around the dining room table. In the corner by the bay window was a biggish cardboard box labeled "Fragile! Do Not Drop!" Atop the box was the old jackknife from the junk drawer.

His heart pounding, Eric opened the main blade and zipped it across the paper tape sealing the top of the box. Inside the shipping box, hidden under wads of brown paper padding, were several smaller boxes.

The largest of the boxes had a label that read, "Parabolic Newtonian astronomical mirror, 64 inches focal length, F8." Eric's hands were shaking as he carefully slit the sealing tape with the jackknife. Inside, between layers of foam, was an 8" glass disk perhaps an inch thick or a little more, showing his astonished face in its perfectly reflecting surface.

His father stood behind him. "You needed a distraction. Sometimes things don't work out. Most of the time, they do. And when you find yourself somewhere in the middle, stay busy."

Eric guided the knife through the tape on the other boxes. A diagonal mirror, a spider mount, an eyepiece holder, and three Kellner eyepieces. Freeze-dried telescope! Just add plywood, pipe fittings, and elbow grease!

"Wow. Dad, thanks. I—"

"Welcome. Now get to work."

"I will. And I'll…um…I'll make you proud."

His father clapped his shoulder. "I'm already proud. Make me prouder."

15

Two Years Later
Saturday, August 10th, 1968

It was almost 200 miles from Arlington Heights to Mauston, Wisconsin. The Lunds had set out early. Lisa was still fast asleep against a pillow in the back seat. Eric stared out the Impala wagon's rear window and let his thoughts wander, as the dawn light rose to full sun.

His life was changing shape. He had graduated at the top of his eighth grade class, and in a few weeks would begin high school. Eric himself was changing shape. This past spring he turned 14, and had a growth spurt that took him from 5'7" to 5'11". He now towered over his mother, and was gaining on his 6'2" father. Weight-lifting at the YMCA was broadening his arms and chest. His parents had warned him of a whole raft of emotional hazards to be encountered when puberty hit him with full force. He had faced them all down.

Highs and lows, sure. A certain moodiness that got in the way of concentration here and there. Besides, the girls at his school were changing shape too. Skinny little girls were becoming shapely young women, and triggering responses girls had never triggered in him before. He had developed a strange fascination with Cathy Zdenek, the smartest girl in his class. She'd caught him looking at her more than once, and raised one eyebrow at him. If he ever worked up the courage to talk to her, he intended to ask her how she did that, and what it meant.

His father reminded him regularly how proud of Eric he was. It surprised Eric how much strength he took from that.

Eric's skills, knowledge, and passions were changing shape. He had built a telescope the previous year that showed him objects in the night sky that made him gasp. He studied computing and electronics in library books, and built a flip-flop circuit of the type the books said lay at the heart of the big machines that kept civilization running. His father introduced him to a young man at his company who sat Eric down in front of a terminal, and showed him how to write simple programs on the IBM computer in the glass-walled room. The idea caught fire in him, and he could not spend enough time reading about and imagining what he could do with access to a computer.

Every so often, Eric thought of the skinny little girl with a big smile he had met two years before. His evening prayers included a line, "Bless Charlene, and please send her someone to love," which he said even over the remembered pain of losing her. He had given her his solemn promise that he would always wish the best for her. She clearly wanted a boy to love, and he could not be that boy. *Lunds did not break promises.* So he prayed for someone strong, kind, and interesting to love her.

An insight caught him up short: Maybe she hadn't answered his letters because God had answered his prayers. If so, well… yes. So be it. *Amen.*

Hey, Eric," his father said, getting back into the car after registering at the campground. "They're not here. I asked."

Eric blinked his way out of reverie. He wasn't surprised. Charlene's family hadn't been there the summer before, either. "That's ok, dad." He had his telescope, and a whole list of deep-sky objects to search for. Plus a stack of library books about computers. The week would go fast.

Only a minute later, crowned by the boxy plywood tube of Eric's telescope, the Impala pulled into the same familiar campsite where they had stayed the past two years. Eric and Lisa got out and sniffed the wonderful pine smell from the canopy of trees above them. Lisa was eight now, and a formidable student at St. James. "I'll always love this place," she said.

Eric was of two minds about it. There was now—and there were memories. As his father had told him a few too many times, Lunds chose their futures, and were the masters of their emotions. So why couldn't he shake off the weight of those memories?

Dumb question. He remembered his first haircut, his first bike, his first train ride, and many other firsts. And he remembered Charlene.

Hey, there was a *lot* of Wisconsin. Maybe he could huddle with his father and find another campground, someplace with dark skies, bright stars, and fewer tears—

Somewhere nearby, Lisa let out a whoop of delight. Eric looked up from pulling suitcases across the tailgate of the Impala. He spun around and saw two girls racing down the campground road toward him.

Moments later, Charlene stood in front of him, in a white sleeveless sundress and white leather thong sandals, her nails bright red, a yellow flower in her hair over one ear. "Omigod, you're here! You're really here!" she said, a broad smile on her face. "And I'm gonna need a *ladder!*"

Charlene's sunstreaked chestnut hair now hung down to her waist. Eric held out his hands. She took them, and pulled herself toward him. "I guess now I have to hold you in even *higher* regard!"

Joyful astonishment was drowning out all other feelings. Eric felt dizzy for a moment. He had no idea what to say. "Um—"

She put her index finger to his lips. "No more 'ums'. *Ever.* Say what you mean or be quiet."

"I missed you."

"Better. And mutual." A long moment passed in silence. Charlene reached around Eric's back and pulled him close. "We've got *so* much to talk about!"

"We do."

Marianne and Lisa stood beside them. Marianne made a show of tapping her foot on the soft earth."Hey, Shar, c'mon, get it over with."

"Over? There is no 'over.'" Charlene stood on tiptoe and placed a lingering kiss on Eric's lips.

Eric looked around. "We have to be careful about—"

"No, we don't." Charlene began beckoning to someone on the road. A man and a woman walked toward them, hand-in-hand, smiling. Marianne ran toward them, took the woman's free hand, and pulled them over the forest loam toward Eric. Charlene laughed. "Eric, this is my real mom, Sarah Orzech, and her husband Mike Orzech. Mom, dad, this is Eric Lund."

Eric's eyes widened. Composure again took a few seconds. *Lunds are the masters of their emotions.*

"I'm now Marianne Orzech," Marianne said with a proud turn of voice.

"Finally I get to meet you," Mrs. Orzech said, and squeezed Eric's outstretched hand. "There've been some changes…"

At last Eric found his smile. *Obviously.*

"Eric. Very glad to meet you." Mr. Orzech shook his hand.

Charlene was bouncing on her toes in excitement. "I belong to them now. Marianne does too. I'm Charlene Orzech!"

"Claire hit me with a cutting board and broke my arm," Marianne said. "They arrested her—"

Charlene put her arm around her sister. "Not now, Mare. This is a happy time. Eric, it's all better. James divorced Claire. He moved to Canada. Mom got custody of both of us. It's a long story. And it's for later. I want your folks to meet my folks. I want us all…to belong to each other."

"We live in Evanston now," Marianne said.

Eric's mouth fell open. "Evanston! That means—"

Charlene grinned. "That means I can see you a lot more often than every two years!"

Eric looked to one side, trying to remember the transit maps his father kept on the kitchen bookshelf. "—I can take the train there!"

Eric's parents rounded the Impala from where they'd been spreading out their old blue tent, Jack with his hand out. "Mike, Sarah, Jack Lund. My wife Marcia. Your girls are amazing! Sit down, I've got cold beer. Hey, we should do a big barbecue together! Whaddaya say?"

Mr. Orzech shook his hand. "Sounds terrific. Charlene told us all about you, and how you encouraged her art. It was a bad time for her. I owe you. Sarah, hey, a two-family meal. Sound good?"

"Great big *yeah!*" Mrs. Orzech came over and shook Jack's hand, and gave Eric's mother a quick hug. "Charlene wouldn't stop talking about Eric. She said her family always stayed here the middle two weeks in August. We agreed to come back and see if you'd be here. I'm not much of a camper, but we'll learn as we go."

Charlene grabbed Eric's T-shirt sleeve and pulled him off toward the trees, an exasperated look on her face. "I told you to write to me, you bum!" she hissed, half under her breath.

Eric frowned. "I did. Six times. About Halloween I gave up. I figured you found another boyfriend."

"Yeah, like *that's* going to happen!" Charlene fell silent, and looked off into the pines. "Oh. Wait. Claire always brought in the mail. I'll bet she dumped your letters in the trash. Eric, I'm sorry. She snapped. She's living with her sister in Oshkosh, under court supervision. She barely escaped a prison term."

"Why did your stepfather move to Canada?"

Charlene looked down, and wrung her hands together. "He's not my stepfather. He's my real father."

Eric was aghast. "You mean, when your mom was fifteen…"

"Yes. He had sex with his niece and got her pregnant. That's a crime called 'statutory rape'. When Claire found out, it was the beginning of the end."

Eric looked toward the picnic table, where his father was cracking beers all around. Marianne was showing two shiny bracelets to Lisa. His mother and Mrs. Orzech were sitting at the picnic table, chatting about the various complications of camping. "How's your new stepfather?"

"He's wonderful. He hugs me. He listens to me. He tells me he's proud of me."

Eric grinned. Mr. Orzech sounded a lot like his own father. Could whole families become friends, all at once? That would be *way* beyond wonderful. "Good fathers do all that. He's your real father now."

"Yes! He is! And he told me he would do everything in his power to help me become a commercial artist. He works for IBM. He took me downtown and introduced me to IBM's publications staff at his office. They spent an afternoon with me. I drew them, and they hung my drawing on the wall! They explained what they do. A lot of commercial art is publishing, designing how pages look, and so on. One of the artists promised me that she would answer any questions about art or publishing, and gave me her business card." She touched her forehead to his shoulder. "Eric, everything's falling into place. It's hard to believe it could all work out this well. I can tell you were praying for me. Thank you."

Eric reached his arms around her. "I'm glad, though when I didn't hear back from you I was actually praying for God to send you a boy to love."

Charlene looked in Eric's eyes and stretched up on tiptoe to give him a quick kiss. "He did."

POSTSCRIPT: Charlene Sophia Orzech married Eric John Lund on August 11, 1979. They have twin sons, Peter and Paul. In 2013 Charlene sold the publishing company she founded, Complete Sentences LLC, for six million dollars. Eric retired from IBM in 2019 and built a computer-controlled observatory in southern Arizona, which he uses to hunt for comets, and to teach his four grandchildren about the stars.

ABOUT THE AUTHOR

Jeff Duntemann has written professionally since 1974, in both science fiction/fantasy and technical nonfiction. His early work in both areas reflects his experience as a programmer for Xerox in the 1970s and 1980s. His stories have appeared in *Isaac Asimov's Science Fiction Magazine, Omni,* the *Orbit* and *Nova* anthology series, and several standalone print anthologies. Two of his short stories have appeared on the final Hugo Awards ballot.

On the nonfiction side, he has worked as a technical editor for Ziff-Davis Publishing and Borland International, launched and edited two print magazines for programmers, and has twenty technical books to his credit, including the bestselling *Assembly Language Step By Step.* He wrote the "Structured Programming" column in *Dr. Dobb's Journal* for four years, and published technical articles in many magazines. He co-founded and ran editorial for The Coriolis Group, which became Arizona's largest book publisher in 1998.

After retiring from technical publishing, Jeff resumed his career as an indie SF author. Most of his fiction involves human-class artificial intelligence. His first novel, *The Cunning Blood,* appeared in hardcover in 2005. All his fiction titles are available through Kindle, in both ebook and paperback editions. Outside of writing and publishing, Jeff's interests include programming, electronics, amateur radio (callsign K7JPD), telescopes, history, psychology, and kites. Jeff lives in Scottsdale, Arizona with his wife Carol and two bichon frise dogs.

Hard SF Action-Adventure at Its Best

Framed for murder by Eath's world government, Peter Novilio is offered his freedom in exchange for a reconnaisance mission to the surface of Hell, Earth's escape-proof prison planet. Hell is infected with a nanobug that eats electrical conductors, making computation and spaceflight impossible. There is a way back, known only to his grim mission partner, Gayle Shreve.

But Peter has a secret too: In his bloodstream he carries the Sangruse Device, an outlawed nanotech AI of fearsome power, with its own reasons for visiting Hell. Peter soon realizes that he is a pawn in a covert war among Earth, Hell's ingenious inmates, and the deadly mechanism in his veins. For as fearsome as it is, the Sangruse Device itself is afraid—and the fates of whole worlds would depend on the threat that the Cunning Blood had discovered outside of space and time.

See Amazon for both ebook and trade paperback formats

"[Jeff Duntemann] returns with an ambitious, polished tale of intrigue, nanotechnology, and something that sounds a lot like mysticism...This one has a decent chance of ending up on award ballots." —Tom Easton, *Analog*

"The book is absolutely *au courant*, and actually extends the Great Work of SF in several unexpected directions. Like most ambitiously sprawling *sui generis* books, this one delivers the sense—as with the work of the recently departed Charles Harness—that the author has chucked every idea he had during the writing of the novel into the pot."   —Paul Di Filippo, *Science Fiction Weekly*

"Whether your interest is in scientific ideas, widescreen action, or sheer flights of imagination, you will find much to enjoy in *The Cunning Blood*. I look forward eagerly to Duntemann's future work." —David Hebblethwaite, *SFSite*

For More SF in the Grand Tradition...

...pick up *Cold Hands and Other Stories*, the newest collection of Jeff Duntemann's short SF and fantasy. This volume includes Jeff's first published story ("Our Lady of the Endless Sky") and the Hugo-nominated "Cold Hands." Three stories take place on Valinor, the Drumlins World: "Drumlin Boilor," "Drumlin Wheel," and "Roddie." As a bonus, there's a new excerpt from *The Cunning Blood*, Jeff's rollicking hard SF action saga of nanotech AI, and a break-out from a prison planet where a bacteria-sized nanotech bug prevents all things electronic from working. Don't miss it!

In This Volume:

- "Cold Hands"   *Nominated for the Hugo Award*
- "Our Lady of the Endless Sky"
- "Inevitability Sphere"
- "Whale Meat"
- "Born Again, with Water"
- "Drumlin Boiler"
- "Drumlin Wheel"
- "Roddie"
- ...and a new excerpt from his novel *The Cunning Blood*

"These stories convey a warmth and generosity of spirit, and an enthusiastic embrace of technology as a means to improve upon the best of mankind."
--Jon Mollison, Castalia House blog

"All told, a rich collection of short stories that you'd expect to be the work of half a dozen authors. A wide range of ideas, varying styles, varying outlooks on the universe...Highly recommended. --Goodreads

Magic and Monsters Vs. Software and AIs

Having cheated a magician out of ten nuggets of pure magic in a rigged card game, spellbender Bartholomew Stypek needs a place to hide. With his anarchic familiar spirit Pickles and the ill-won magical Opportunities, Stypek leaps blindly across universes, hoping to be dropped someplace far away and without magic... and lands in the break room of a small advertising agency in Upstate New York.

Because our universe doesn't support spirits, Pickles manifests as the local equivalent: AI software in the agency's heavily networked copier. She wanders into a nearby corporate network looking for allies, and finds a virtual universe where AIs live and train for jobs as AI products. Stypek, mistaken for a penniless CS intern, is taken in by the ad agency's copywriter. Expecting the usual suspicion and contempt, he is humbled by the kindness he's shown, and one by one uses the stolen Opportunities to help his new friends with their problems.

But Jrikk the magician isn't so easily thwarted. Soon Stypek, Pickles, and both their human and virtual friends must fight for their lives against the evil force sent to retrieve Stypek to the magician's dungeons.

Kindle EBook $2.99 Trade Paperback $12.99

"*Ten Gentle Opportunities* represents the best that science fiction and fantasy have to offer. It blends the two genres in a clever and original way. It presents near future tech that is plausible, delightful, and a little scary. Best of all, it provides an exuberant and unapologetic adventure that incorporates action, violence, romance, and robots in ways that are both exciting, fun to read, and even a little bit educational."

—Jon Mollison, Seagull Rising

Two Short Novels of the Drumlins World In One Volume

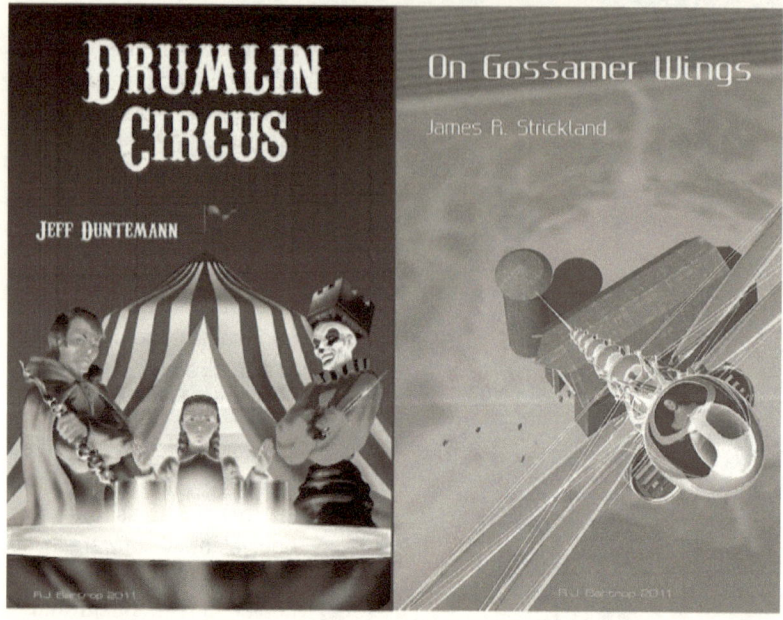

Step up to the pillars in front of the big bowl of gray dust, tap the pillars 256 times in any pattern, and *something* appears in the bowl. What? *Almost anything.* This is the Drumlins World, an alien planet where the aliens have gone, leaving their replicator machines behind, still working, still capable of producing 10^{77} different things—one for every atom in the universe! Here are two short novels by Drumlins creator Jeff Duntemann and *Brass and Steel* author Jim Strickland:

• In *Drumlin Circus*, a circus master attempts to free his wife from the shadowy Bitspace Institute, with the help of his bodyguard clowns (one a former Institute man with a grudge against the organization) and a preteen girl with a whistle drumlin that can make other drumlins, animals, and even human beings obey her. Intrigue, steam, smilodons, airships, and nonstop action!

• *On Gossamer Wings* tells the story of a teen girl who cannot speak, but has a strange talent allowing her to find exactly the drumlin she wants among the 10^{77} possibilities in the Thingmakers. Her farm town neighbors hold her in contempt, and she struggles to realize her dream of building a drumlin flying machine before the Bitspace Institute fully comprehends the breadth of her powers.

Kindle EBook $2.99 Trade Paperback $12.99

The Best Epoxy Glue
in the Known Galaxy...

...comes from Scattershot, home of a newly-contacted alien race that manufactures the glue in their ample digestive tracts. Having dropped a snooty alien-contact anthropologist on Scattershot to establish a relationship with the Rockchompers, starship *Richard M. Nixon* and its crew return two years later on a trade mission. The corporations of Earth's Tripartisan Economic Combine are eager to buy the Rockchompers' glue. Vincent Icehall, the starship's young shuttle pilot, has little to do during the mission but hang out with the alien community's jester and village idiot. Icehall can't pronounce the alien's name and dubs him "Turkey," but slowly realizes that Turkey is anything but. Ignoring all of Turkey's warnings to leave the planet immediately, Icehall stumbles on a plot by the anthropologist and the Rockchompers' chieftain to steal the *Nixon*'s shuttle for use as a weapon of war.

Dedicated to Keith Laumer and very much in the wry style of his Retief adventures, *Firejammer* is a tribute to the man who taught a whole generation of SF authors how to write funny aliens.

Kindle EBook $2.99 Trade Paperback $6.99

"If Hal Clement had written for *Planet Stories* he might have produced a story like *Firejammer*. This is a light-hearted action adventure story with aliens that are truly alien -- not just humans in funny suits."

—Amazon

Meet Larry: He's Your Worst Nightmare's Worst Nightmare

By day, Larry Kettelkamp is an IT guy at a collapsing industrial bakery. By night, he wages a 30-year running war on nightmares. For he discovered decades earlier that nightmares are deliberately created by strange creatures called *archons*, who drop bad dreams into sleeping minds and then feast on the anger or terror they engender. Larry enters nightmares, banishes the archons responsible for them, and vaccinates the dreamers against that nightmare using a mysterious symbol found on a tomb wall centuries before. After Larry learns how to destroy archons (and not merely banish them from dreams) the boss archon, who styles himself as the Demiurge of ancient Persian myth, comes looking for him. Larry's war turns hot as the Demiurge sends a human death cult after him, wielding dark magic and ancient psychoactive poisons. But Larry has allies: a bored title search agent, a witch and a lightworker, two teen-age prodigies, the spirit of a Victorian engineer, and Lord Air, the Alpha of every dreaming dog on Earth. Together they descend to the very center of the collective unconscious for a final battle that could mean death and madness, or the end of nightmares forever.

Kindle EBook $3.99   Trade Paperback $12.99

"I love when a fantasy or sci-fi author takes things in a new direction, and this story does that in spades. Adventure, fun characters, and quantum dream manipulation with living dream entities brings a fun new different and unique perspective."

—Amazon